T0029477

PRAISE FOR CHAD ZUNKER

Family Money

"The action barrels along to a shocking conclusion . . . Zunker knows how to keep the reader hooked."

—*Publishers Weekly*

An Equal Justice

HARPER LEE PRIZE FOR LEGAL FICTION FINALIST

"A deftly crafted legal thriller of a novel by an author with a genuine knack for a reader-engaging narrative storytelling style . . ."

—*Midwest Book Review*

"A gripping thriller with a heart, *An Equal Justice* hits the ground running . . . The chapters flew by, with surprises aplenty and taut writing. A highly recommended read that introduces a lawyer with legs."

—Crime Thriller Hound

"In *An Equal Justice*, author Chad Zunker crafts a riveting legal thriller . . . *An Equal Justice* not only plunges readers into murder and conspiracy involving wealthy power players but also immerses us in the crisis of homelessness in our country."

—*The Big Thrill*

"A thriller with a message. A pleasure to read. Twists I didn't see coming. I read it in one sitting."

—Robert Dugoni, #1 Amazon bestselling author of *My Sister's Grave*

"Taut, suspenseful, and action packed with a hero you can root for, Zunker has hit it out of the park with this one."

—Victor Methos, bestselling author of *The Neon Lawyer*

An Unequal Defense

"In Zunker's solid sequel to 2019's *An Equal Justice* . . . he sustains a disciplined focus on plot and character. John Grisham fans will appreciate this familiar but effective tale."

—*Publishers Weekly*

Runaway Justice

"[In the] engrossing third mystery featuring attorney David Adams . . . Zunker gives heart and hope to his characters. There are no lulls in this satisfying story of a young runaway in trouble."

—*Publishers Weekly*

THE WIFE YOU KNOW

ALSO BY CHAD ZUNKER

Stand-Alones

Family Money

All He Has Left

David Adams Series

An Equal Justice

An Unequal Defense

Runaway Justice

Sam Callahan Series

The Tracker

Shadow Shepherd

Hunt the Lion

THE WIFE YOU KNOW

CHAD ZUNKER

This is a work of fiction. Names, characters, organizations, places, events, and incidents are either products of the author's imagination or are used fictitiously. Otherwise, any resemblance to actual persons, living or dead, is purely coincidental.

Text copyright © 2024 by Chad Zunker
All rights reserved.

No part of this book may be reproduced, or stored in a retrieval system, or transmitted in any form or by any means, electronic, mechanical, photocopying, recording, or otherwise, without express written permission of the publisher.

Published by Thomas & Mercer, Seattle

www.apub.com

Amazon, the Amazon logo, and Thomas & Mercer are trademarks of Amazon.com, Inc., or its affiliates.

ISBN-13: 9781662515514 (hardcover)
ISBN-13: 9781662515491 (paperback)
ISBN-13: 9781662515507 (digital)

Cover design by Rex Bonomelli
Cover image: © Bulgac, © Wirestock, © Thomas Barwick / Getty

Printed in the United States of America

First edition

To Charlotte, whose magic touch helps bring my stories to life

PROLOGUE

Ashley Driskell stared at the smoke-filled Colorado sky. She was lying on her back on the dry grass, her eyes stinging, her skin feeling like it was on fire—just like the day-care facility she'd entered and barely escaped a few seconds ago. But she thought she was basically okay. She'd rolled four times to be sure nothing on her was still aflame. Coughing repeatedly, she found it difficult to breathe. She kept gasping. She'd inhaled a lot of smoke. But she'd gotten all the kids out of the classroom; she was sure of it. She'd searched every corner of the room before crawling out the same broken window as the children—a window she'd shattered with one of Luke's golf clubs, which she'd grabbed from the back of her SUV.

Ashley could hear sirens wailing now. She looked over toward the small parking lot. Her vision was a bit blurry, but she could make out a Vail Fire Department engine arriving with several police cars and other emergency vehicles. Thank God. There was a big crowd of day-care workers, along with a large group of frightened kids, all standing in the parking lot outside the school. Many of the children looked to be the same age as Joy, her daughter, who had just celebrated her third birthday. They were all staring wide-eyed at the fire-engulfed school building.

Ashley had no idea how the building had caught on fire. She'd only been driving by, on the way to Raitman Art Galleries to drop off a new painting she'd completed, when she spotted what looked like a sudden explosion to her right, followed by a mass of flames. She'd responded on instinct. That had always been her nature—to go where others wouldn't to make a difference. To step into the gap for those in need. Especially children. An emotional reflex born from the cold reality that no one had been there for her as she bounced from one foster home to the next those first fourteen years of her life. Not until Janny. However, putting herself in harm's way for other people had cost her dearly once before. She'd lost everything.

Ashley thought of Joy. *Well, not everything.*

She'd also gained the only thing that mattered.

Police officers began pushing the growing group of people farther back from the building. Ashley noticed several of the adults with their cell phones out and pointed at the facility, probably taking videos as tall flames licked the August sky and a heavy cloud of black smoke blotted out the afternoon sun. She suddenly felt a tinge of concern sweep through her. Had any of them taken video of her? There had been a couple of other panicked women standing around when she'd arrived, and they'd all noticed what looked like a group of trapped schoolchildren in the window of the last classroom in the building. But Ashley had been the only one to make a move.

Could what she had just done somehow expose her?

She was probably being paranoid. She'd hoped that marrying Luke this past year would finally squash that fear and bring on a renewed sense of safety and security. She was desperate for it. And Luke was so kind and patient. He embraced all her odd idiosyncrasies. He didn't push her out of her comfort zone. He was okay with the way she concealed so much about herself. Her past. She loved him in a way that she had never thought she'd be able to love again. She had felt completely safe with him—but only for a short time. Like a wild beast relentlessly hunting her down, the fear always came roaring back. It was what she thought about every time she looked at her precious Joy. It was the first thing she thought about when waking up in the morning and the last thing she thought about before closing her eyes at night.

The beast was always back there. Prowling. Stalking.

Threatening to take the only thing that mattered.

ONE

I felt panic punch me hard in the gut and steal my breath. I didn't get Ashley's erratic voice mail until two hours after she'd left it, while I was walking off the private plane at Eagle County Regional Airport, just outside Vail. I'd been asleep for most of the flight back from Palo Alto. After getting up well before sunrise that morning for a quick day trip out to California to meet with my partners at the software company we'd started, I was completely exhausted on the way back. I regretted sleeping now. Her words woke me up quick.

"Hey, it's Ashley . . ." Cough, cough. "I'm headed to the hospital right now in an ambulance. There was a fire, Luke, but . . ." Cough, cough. "I think . . . I think I'm okay. Joy is . . . I don't . . . You're probably already on the plane. Just call me when you get this, and I'll explain everything. Love you."

I could hear the ambulance's siren in the background of her message. A fire? Joy? Was it our home? I quickly dialed up my wife's number, my hands beginning to tremble. The phone rang four times and went straight to an automated voice mail. Ashley had never taken the time to create her own personalized greeting. When I first met her, she hadn't even owned a cell phone. As someone who was always connected in numerous ways, I found this baffling—*and* so refreshing. I cursed, called her again. Same result. So I began hustling through the small airport terminal, feeling the panic inside me grow.

Hitting the sidewalk outside the airport, I ran toward the short-term parking lot, my leather briefcase in one hand, my blue sport coat clutched in the other. I only wore sport coats while attending meetings. I hated getting dressed up. Most days, I worked at home in a T-shirt and blue jeans. I found my white Range Rover where I'd left it that morning and quickly climbed inside. I was racing down I-70 toward Vail a few minutes later. It was normally about a thirty-minute drive, but I planned to make it much quicker. I presumed Ashley had meant the hospital in Vail. She'd had no plans to leave the area today, as far as I knew.

I tried her cell phone again. She still didn't answer. That made me feel uneasy. Ashley had said she was okay, but was she really? Had she just said that so I wouldn't freak out? She'd done that once before when I was traveling. Joy had fractured her arm on the playground. Ashley had told me over the phone that she'd only gotten a "boo-boo" and was okay. I'd found out the severity of it when I got home and saw the cast. Ashley had explained she didn't want me freaking out and leaving my meeting early. She was right—I would've bolted straight for the airport. Joy already felt like my own daughter. She had accepted me way before Ashley ever came around to it, and we'd developed a special bond in a short amount of time.

I scrambled to find the number for Vail Health Hospital on my phone while trying not to swerve off the highway.

A friendly female voice answered. "Vail Health, how may I direct your call?"

"I'm looking for my wife, Ashley Driskell. I believe she was brought in by ambulance a couple of hours ago."

"Yes, Mr. Driskell, she's here."

"What happened? Is she okay?"

"Let me see if I can get a doctor for you. Please hold."

I pressed my foot down harder on the gas pedal. I was nearing ninety-five miles per hour, zipping around slower-moving traffic. My heart hammered in my chest. I took several deep breaths, ran my fingers through my wavy hair, tried to calm myself down. I didn't need to have an anxiety attack right now. I used to have them weekly. But I hadn't had one since I met Ashley a year ago. I glanced out my window at the Rocky Mountains. They were always calming and peaceful to me. They were the reason I'd chosen this place when starting my life over eighteen months ago. I'd had to escape California after my first wife's tragic death. It had become too painful to constantly drive by all our favorite restaurants and hangouts, and I'd quickly grown weary of running into our friends and always getting the sad head tilt as people asked how I was doing. I no longer wanted to return to the beautiful home Jill and I had renovated together. I couldn't even walk into the nursery we'd spent months preparing for our child.

A widower at thirty. A baby girl I never got to hold.

Nothing can quite prepare you for something so devastating.

Especially when you have only yourself to blame.

My thoughts returned to Ashley. I had never expected to be married again so soon. I certainly hadn't gone looking for it. I was still struggling with grief and battling guilt. But I was admittedly lonely. Money doesn't solve loneliness. In many ways, it can isolate you even more. After Jill died, I'd also made a commitment to myself to seize the moment, knowing how fast life can change. Go skydiving. Eat new, strange foods. Take more risks. I hadn't anticipated one of those risks would come in the form of another woman. But Ashley was unlike anyone I'd ever met. While younger than me by six years, she had a maturity about her that reached well beyond her age. She was so different from me. She seemed so healthily detached from the materialistic pulls of the modern world. She didn't place much value in life's luxuries. She was never too impressed with the $15 million house I'd purchased in the heart of Vail. She'd been almost embarrassed to live in it—even though she had made it much homier since moving in after we were married. Ashley didn't seem to care what others thought. She had zero interest in social media. She was *very* private. She didn't want me posting pictures of her and Joy. Ashley was content living in her own little world. Just focused on her art and Joy. And now me. I loved that about her. So much of my life had been about pleasing others and proving myself—the dirt-poor kid from a South Texas trailer park who had made himself into a huge success.

Ashley was a refuge for me. I could not lose her.

"Mr. Driskell?" The same receptionist was back on the phone. "We've had another emergency. I'm sorry, but Dr. Longview will have to call you right back."

"Can you just tell me if my wife is okay?"

"I'm not allowed to comment on the status of our patients." She paused, lowered her voice. "But I can tell you that your wife is a hero. What she did to save those kids was incredible."

"What kids? What're you talking about?"

"You don't know?"

"I don't know anything!" I blurted out.

I felt my neck growing hot from frustration. I needed to know what the hell had happened or else I was going to lose it.

"Sir, your wife ran into a burning building. It's all over social media."

TWO

I hurried up to the sliding glass doors of Vail Health Hospital a few minutes later. I noticed two Denver TV news–affiliate vans parked in the circle drive-through right outside the facility. I still had not heard back from the doctor, which was infuriating. This only fed my fear that something horrific had happened to my wife. A burning building? Saving kids? How badly had she been hurt? Hearing that my wife was a hero had not helped.

The four-story hospital building was pristine, just like most others in this affluent town. I'd been inside the facility only once before, when I'd cracked my collarbone last ski season while taking a black diamond trail a little too vigorously. Entering the building, I spotted what looked like two TV reporters in the main lobby—a man and a woman—huddled with two camera guys, based off the gear at their feet. They all glanced over at me. I ignored them and headed straight for a sleek, modern reception desk. A fiftysomething redhead with a name tag that said "Brenda" sat behind it. She seemed to know who I was just by the distraught look on my face. Probably the same woman I'd been on the phone with a few minutes earlier.

She stood. "Mr. Driskell?"

I nodded. "Where is my wife?"

Upon hearing the receptionist use my name, the two reporters hustled over in my direction, as if they'd been waiting for my arrival.

The woman got to me first. "Mr. Driskell, can we talk to you about your wife?"

I furrowed my brow. "What about her?"

"Your wife saved those kids," the male reporter chimed in. "She's a local hero. We really want to speak with her. And to you. It's an amazing story!"

"I'd like to speak with her first," I snapped, feeling like everyone but me already knew what had happened with Ashley.

Brenda quickly came out from behind the desk and put her hand on my arm. "Right this way. Dr. Longview is waiting for you."

She guided me down a hallway, away from the aggressive TV reporters—who were still calling after me—and toward the emergency department. Brenda pushed through a door, and a gray-haired doctor in scrubs with a clipboard in his hands looked up from a nearby counter. Noticing my arrival, he immediately walked over to me.

"Mr. Driskell?"

"Yes. Luke Driskell."

"I'm Dr. Longview. My apologies about not getting to the phone earlier. I had another emergency pop up right when you called. But listen, Ashley is doing okay. She's resting comfortably now. Mostly second-degree burns on her arms and neck, possibly a couple of spots I'd designate third degree. She's also suffering from smoke inhalation, so we have her on a steady supply of oxygen to try to help. We need to keep her overnight to monitor her upper airway for any potential issues. If that clears up, she should be fine to go home at some point tomorrow."

I felt relief pour through me. "What exactly happened?"

"You haven't heard?"

I shook my head. "No, I was on a plane. I drove here as soon as I departed, after getting a brief voice mail from my wife."

"Well, sir, your wife came upon a day-care facility that had caught on fire. I'm not sure how just yet. I've heard possibly a gas leak exploding. Ashley spotted children that were trapped in a classroom. She broke a window and helped them to all get out safely. She is truly remarkable."

Brenda was still standing there behind me. "Would you like to see the video, Mr. Driskell?"

I turned around. "There's a video?"

"Yes. A bystander recorded it."

She handed me her phone, which displayed a cell phone video that had been posted on Twitter from the *Vail News* account. The tag read: Local woman heroically saves schoolchildren from fire. I pressed the play button and watched what was clearly Ashley running toward a brick building engulfed in flames. She was wearing the same denim overalls and white tennis shoes she always wore when painting. Her long dark hair was pulled up into its usual messy bun on top of her head. It looked like she was carrying something in her hand. I squinted. Was it one of my golf clubs? I'd asked her to drop a couple of them by a sporting-goods store to be regripped.

Ashley stepped in front of a glass window, waving her hands wildly. It looked like there were kids inside the room. Ashley then took a swing with the golf club. The window shattered. A billow of smoke poured out of the room, straight into my wife's face. Ashley took several more swings to clear glass shards away from the windowsill. Then she climbed inside and began lifting kids up through the window, to freedom. I counted eight of them before she stopped. Ashley didn't climb out the window herself until thirty seconds later, when she collapsed onto the grass. The phone pivoted to show the kids all running toward the parking lot. Then the person who'd been recording began running after the kids, and the video stopped.

I could feel my chest pounding again, even though I knew Ashley was okay. It was one thing to hear about what she'd done, but it was another thing to see it with my own eyes. My wife always put others first.

It was one of the things I loved about her. She had a big heart for helping those in need. She'd get up early several Sundays a month to drive into Denver and serve the homeless breakfast at a downtown church. She volunteered to be an activity buddy with Caregiver Connections, a local nonprofit that paired seniors in need with someone willing to take them on outings to the grocery store or the library, or just to play board games with them. She'd helped build several homes with Habitat for Humanity—something I had enjoyed doing with her this past year. But today's act was stunning. She'd risked her own life.

"The video has gone viral," the receptionist explained. "It's already been viewed over one hundred thousand times in only a couple of hours. Every time I check, the count has gone up by tens of thousands. I guess everyone is sharing it. It's amazing. The Denver TV reporters out there in the lobby must've seen it, jumped in their vans, and driven straight out here."

I turned to the doctor. "Is everyone okay at the day-care center?"

"Yes," he confirmed. "Everyone got out. Thanks to your wife."

"Good. Can I see her now?"

"Of course. This way."

I followed him down another short hallway, around a corner; then he offered a hand toward a hospital room.

"She's been sleeping off and on," the doctor said. "We medicated her heavily so we could poke, prod, and address all her burns. She's comfortable now but will be sore for a while as her wounds heal."

"Okay, thanks."

I pushed through the door, hesitantly entered the hospital room. I was unsure how I'd feel seeing Ashley in this condition. Was she in pain? How much was she suffering? Had her face also been burned? Would she be permanently scarred? I took a deep breath, let it out slowly, and stepped fully into the room. Ashley was lying in a hospital bed, a white sheet pulled up to her waist. Her eyes were closed. I could see she was in a blue hospital gown. Both of her arms were exposed above the sheet and covered in white bandages. There was also a small white bandage on the left side of her neck. But her face was left untouched—other than a small oxygen mask covering her nose and mouth.

I stepped up close to her bedside. I could see dark smudges at the edges of her face—probably soot from the fire. This reminded me of the first time we met, the previous summer at the annual Outdoor Arts Festival over in the Arrabelle at Vail Square. More than fifty artists had been showcasing paintings, photography, sculpture, jewelry, wood and metal works, and so much more. Ashley had been one of them. I remember she had paint splatter on her face. I'd thought it was cute.

I brushed a strand of her curly dark-brown hair away from her eyes. This woke her up. She looked up at me and gradually smiled. Then she pulled the oxygen mask down to her chin.

"Hey," she said softly, her voice even raspier than usual. I loved her voice. I'd sometimes catch her singing softly while painting, and it always reminded me of listening to Adele. Dark, rich, and raspy.

"Hey back," I replied. It's what we always said. Like saying *I love you* without having to say it. Then I gave her a playful smile. "I thought you were planning to relax today after finishing your new piece."

She offered a small grin. "Change of plans, I guess."

"I guess. I heard what you did. My wife, the hero, they say."

"Hardly."

"I think the parents of those kids would say differently."

"I'm just glad everyone is okay."

"Well, I'm just glad *you're* okay. Is Joy still with Ms. Marie?"

She nodded. "I called and told her you would pick her up later."

Ms. Marie was an elderly neighbor who watched Joy on days when Ashley locked herself in her art studio on the second floor of our home.

"Sorry it took me so long to get here. I was sleeping on the plane. I didn't get your message until I was arriving. Are you feeling okay?"

"I think so. I don't really feel anything right now."

"They have you pumped full of pain meds. The doctor says they want to keep you overnight."

She frowned. "Yeah, he told me that. I just want to go home."

"You need to stay, babe. Let someone take care of you for once."

"Fine," she huffed, rolling her eyes.

"Do you want me to bring Joy up here?"

"No, I don't want her to see me like this in the hospital. I don't even want her to know what happened. It might scare her and give her nightmares."

"That may be hard to prevent."

"Why?" she asked, forehead bunching.

"You haven't heard about the video?"

Her eyes narrowed. "What video?"

"Someone took a video of you saving all those kids. It's apparently all over social media right now and been viewed a hundred thousand times, or something crazy like that. There are even two TV reporters here from Denver that want to interview you. Like I said—my wife, the hero."

I saw a tremor of something flit through her green eyes. Then her face suddenly grew pale, like she might be sick.

"Hey, you okay?" I asked, concerned.

She didn't respond at first. She just kind of stared blankly beyond me, at the ceiling or something, like she was having a difficult time processing what I'd just told her.

"Ash?" I leaned over, breaking her trance. "Do I need to get the doctor?"

She forcefully exhaled, as if she'd been holding her breath for some reason, then looked at me. "Hey, I don't . . . I don't want to talk to any reporters, okay?"

"No problem. Maybe later?"

She shook her head adamantly. "No, not later. Never."

"Oh, okay."

"And I don't want you talking to them, either."

I tilted my head. "Why?"

"I just . . . I don't want to make a big deal out of this, that's all. You know me. I hate being the center of attention. I like my privacy."

"I know, but what you did *was* a big deal."

"Luke, please. No reporters."

She was so resolute it took me off guard.

"Okay, no worries. I'll brush them off."

"Thank you." Her eyes were back on the ceiling, her mind clearly lost somewhere else. She turned to me again. "Will you please go get Joy right now and take her home?"

"Now? I just got here. Joy is fine with Ms. Marie."

"I know. But it would make me feel better. Please, just go get her."

Her breath was still short. Maybe the shock of what had happened today was finally hitting her. I couldn't be sure, but I wanted her to calm down.

"Yes, of course. I'll go get her. You just rest, okay?"

"Call me when you have her home."

"I will. Just take it easy."

I leaned down, kissed her on the lips. She barely kissed me back.

Something had clearly triggered her.

THREE

I pulled up to the modern two-story white stucco house I'd purchased along beautiful Gore Creek, which flowed through the center of town and was hugged closely by well-landscaped walking trails. The ski-in, ski-out home was close to the slopes and within easy walking distance to dozens of restaurants, retail shops, and other venues that made Vail so popular. At more than six thousand square feet, the house had five bedrooms; a heated indoor lap pool; a media room; a gym; and floor-to-ceiling windows nearly everywhere, showing off spectacular views of both the creek below and the mountains above. The place was admittedly ostentatious and so far away from where I'd grown up in Seguin, about thirty miles east of San Antonio. I barely remember my parents, who were both schoolteachers. They were killed by a drunk driver while out cycling together down an isolated country road when I was only four years old. So I'd been raised by my grandfather, who had lived nearby on six desolate acres he'd inherited from his own father.

My grandfather, whom I'd called Pop, had been a former truck driver who survived off a settlement check he got well before I was born, when he mangled his left arm in an accident with his truck trailer. The arm kind of just sat limp next to his body. Pop would drink from sunup to sundown. He wasn't abusive with me or anything. Just absent. And he didn't really know much about raising children since he'd been on the road most of the time during my mom's childhood. Which put me in a tough spot. Kids had been mean to me early on because I began wearing the same clothes to school nearly every day. Pop had only gone to the laundromat once a week, at most, and never bought me new clothes. He'd said he used to wear the same clothes all the time growing up and kids were spoiled these days. He'd told me I could wash them in the sink myself and hang them on a line outside to dry. A bigger classmate had eventually felt sorry for me and given me some of his hand-me-downs. I'd taken them, but I *hated* the feeling. I was ten years old at the time. And I swore to myself right then and there that I would do whatever necessary to get rich.

But the pursuit of money had also cost me dearly.

Sitting there in my car, I thought about my first wife and unborn child. They would likely still be alive if I hadn't been so driven to reach my goal.

I opened the glass garage door and pulled my Range Rover inside. Ashley's gray Mazda SUV was not parked in the garage, and it dawned on me that I'd have to go retrieve it from where she'd likely left it, over by the day-care facility. I would do that first thing in the morning. I'd wanted to buy Ashley a new luxury vehicle as a wedding gift, but she would have none of it—even though her old Mazda had well over a hundred and fifty thousand miles on it and we'd already replaced the brakes, the alternator, and all four tires. She'd said she would drive it until it no longer moved. She was stubborn like that. For her birthday, I'd surprised her with diamond earrings. While grateful at the overture, she'd asked me to return them. Instead, we had made a significant donation to the homeless charity she volunteered with in Denver. There was nothing flashy about her. Recently, she'd started mentioning that maybe the house was too big for just the three of us and hinting that we might want to eventually move into something more *appropriate*.

One thing was certain—Ashley hadn't married me for my money.

I got out of my vehicle, pulled my phone from my pocket. It had been buzzing regularly, as people I knew in the community had begun texting me about the video of Ashley on social media. I knew Ashley didn't want to make a big deal out of what she'd done, but there didn't seem to be any way to stop it. Everyone in town was going to be talking about it the next few days.

Instead of going inside the house, I walked back up the paver driveway and down the tree-lined street, passing by two other modern glass houses before following the front sidewalk to the more traditional cabin-like mountain home that belonged to Ms. Marie. My neighbor was eighty-two but still seemed sharp as a whip. She and her husband had bought their place fifteen years ago, when he'd handed the keys to his investment firm over to his son and retired. He'd tragically had a heart attack and died not long after they moved to Vail. Ms. Marie had stayed and made a good life for herself. She had nine grandkids and six great-grandkids, but none of them were local. Because she loved kids, she looked for opportunities to engage with neighborhood children and be helpful.

I knocked on her wooden front door. Ms. Marie answered, wearing a nurse outfit from days past, comprised of a starched white dress, white cap, white nylons, and white shoes. The tiny woman looked straight out of a '60s hospital. Behind her, I could see my stepdaughter, Joy, standing there in the hallway, dressed up in the doctor's costume we'd gotten her recently for her birthday: long white jacket, stethoscope hanging around her neck, plastic medical kit opened at her feet. There were several Barbie dolls lined up on the hardwood floor in the hallway. Since getting the costume, Joy had wanted to play doctor's office every single time she came over to Ms. Marie's house. And our sweet former-nurse neighbor always happily obliged.

"Luke!" Joy yelled out, running straight to me.

I bent down and scooped her up into my arms. My stepdaughter's spirit matched her name: she was pure joy. A smile that could light up the room. I could see a lot of Ashley in Joy—same button nose, dimpled cheeks, and rounded chin—although her eyes were much darker, and her hair was jet-black and completely straight. I presumed her eyes were like her father's, although I'd never seen a picture of him. Ashley had never been married to the guy, a Chinese art dealer in California. She called him a brief mistake that had produced the greatest blessing. I didn't know much else about him other than his name and that he'd died in a car accident when Ashley was pregnant. Ashley didn't like to talk too much about that period of her life. I hadn't pushed her on it. I'd learned early on that *never* worked with my wife. She talked about things only when she felt ready. Our first couple of dates were mostly me telling her all about myself. I'd had to pry information out of her. I still did.

"Doctor again?" I said to Joy with a smile.

"Yes!" she exclaimed. "Come see my patients."

I put her down, looked over at Ms. Marie. "I hope she's not wearing you out too much."

Ms. Marie kind of giggled. "Not at all. But I will say that I haven't been on my feet this much since I was a real nurse sixty years ago."

I walked over, bent down next to the row of Barbie dolls, and listened as Joy explained why each of them was in the hospital. All the dolls were covered with Band-Aids or had limbs wrapped up in tissue paper.

I patted her on the head. "That's a lot of patients for one doctor."

"I know. But I'm a good doctor."

"No doubt." I smiled and stood again. "Well, we need to wrap it up here at the hospital and go on home."

"Aw, can I stay longer? Please, please?"

"No, honey. We need to let Ms. Marie get some rest."

"Okay." Joy moped but began collecting her dolls.

"I can't thank you enough," I said to Ms. Marie. "You're always a godsend to us."

"I think I look forward to these days as much as Joy."

"That's nice to hear."

"Is Ashley still working on her painting?" Ms. Marie asked.

I'd wondered on the way over if Ms. Marie would know anything about Ashley's situation. The woman was not on social media. But I thought she might have perhaps spoken to a friend on the phone about it. That didn't appear to be the case. And I didn't want to talk about it in front of Joy.

"Not at the moment. She's just busy with something else."

"Well, I sure do love her beautiful paintings."

Ms. Marie had purchased two pieces of art from Ashley and had both hanging in her study.

I carried Joy's pink backpack over my shoulder while we held hands and made the short walk back to our home. While Ashley never made too much fuss over our house, Joy had always loved everything about it. After moving in, Joy swam in the heated indoor lap pool nearly every day for the first month. I had bought her a mermaid tail and all, and she never wanted to take it off. But she'd loved her big bedroom even more than the pool. As a surprise, I'd hired a decorator and had her bedroom painted bright pink and loaded it up with lots of pink sparkle and flair. Whatever would delight a three-year-old girl. I'll never forget Joy's robust smile and explosion of cheer upon entering the bedroom for the first time. I even thought I saw tears in Ashley's eyes at her daughter's priceless reaction.

When I'd met them, Ashley and Joy had been living in a tiny one-bedroom apartment over in Eagle, a town up the road from Vail. They had been sleeping in the same bed. Joy had made a comment to me the day I surprised her with the bedroom that she'd never had her very own room. Ashley casually dismissed it as nonsense, but I'd always wondered if it was true. Ashley had only recently begun selling her pieces at a higher price point—and she only did that because the galleries had told her she had to triple her prices if she ever wanted the town's affluent to show interest. Ashley had worked odd jobs over the years to support herself while painting. Waitressing, coffee shops, bookstores—whatever it took. So I doubted they'd ever been able to afford much more than a one-bedroom apartment.

We entered the house through the garage and stepped into the spacious kitchen, with its massive island that could easily fit ten people around it.

"You hungry?" I asked Joy.

She nodded enthusiastically.

"How hungry?"

"Big hungry! Huge! Like an elephant!"

I laughed. "An elephant? Wow. That is big. Then how about pizza from Blue Moose?"

Her eyes widened. "But Mommy only lets me have pizza on Saturdays."

"Well, Mommy has an overnight tonight. So it's just you and me, kid, until tomorrow." I lowered my voice to a playful whisper. "And I won't tell her if you won't tell her."

Her smile grew even bigger. I'd hoped the offer of pizza would offset any trepidation my stepdaughter might have when hearing that Ashley was going to be gone all night. There had been only two other times when her mother went out of town for an art show and left Joy with me, and we'd had big tears on both occasions. I was trying my best to head that off tonight.

"Pepperoni?" I asked.

"And sausage!"

I matched her smile. "Of course, sausage. How about ice cream, too?"

"Really? Yay!"

"I'll place the order. You go get in your pajamas."

She skipped off down the hallway. It appeared my bribe had worked. I called up delivery for the pizza, turned on the TV in the living room to a national cable news channel, and then poured myself a glass of red wine. After taking my first sip, I nearly spit it out when I suddenly heard my wife's name mentioned on TV. I stepped out of the kitchen and closer to the TV above the fireplace. My mouth dropped open. They were showing the cell phone video of Ashley saving the kids. I couldn't believe it. And they were talking about her: *Ashley Driskell, a painter in Vail, Colorado* . . . Then they showed an up-close photo of Ashley standing with one of her paintings at a recent art show. They must've somehow grabbed the photo off the art gallery's Facebook page. I quickly turned the TV off just as Joy raced back into the room. But my phone started blowing up again. I was now starting to get texts from people I knew from across the country.

I shook my head. This had just turned into something much bigger than a local-hero story. Ashley was not going to be too pleased. I wasn't sure how I was going to shield her from this becoming a media spectacle, but I would try my best. It would probably take a few days of hiding out, but Ashley needed to stay home to allow her wounds to heal anyway.

I again thought about her reaction when she'd first heard about the video. I'd never seen that distant, alarmed look in her eyes.

What had that all been about?

FOUR

My phone began buzzing on my nightstand a few minutes before six the next morning. It took me a moment to come to my senses and remember that my wife was not in bed with me. Where was she? Oh yeah—the fire, the rescue, the hospital. I'd had a strange dream about it during the night. It was like I was there, on-site, watching Ashley go into the burning building to rescue those kids. But this time she never came out. I kept waiting for her to appear through the window, because that's what happened in the video, but she never did. And I couldn't get my legs to move toward the building. Like I was stuck in concrete or something. It was a nightmare. When the firefighters finally put the blaze out, they found no sign of her anywhere inside the building. No burned body. Nothing. My wife was simply gone.

I reached over, pulled my phone closer to my face, the glow blinding me for a second. Speaking of the hospital. The ID said VAIL HEALTH. I wondered if Ashley was calling me from her hospital room. Maybe her cell phone had died. We'd last spoken right before I put Joy down for the night. Ashley had seemed like her usual self when talking to her daughter. But she'd still seemed somewhat distant—or distracted—when speaking to me. I wasn't sure why, but I'd hoped a good night's rest would turn things around. I hadn't mentioned anything to her about her story becoming national news.

"Hello?" I answered, my throat catching from being dry.

"Luke?"

It was not Ashley. It was a man.

"Yes?"

"This is Dr. Longview over at Vail Health."

I sat fully upright in bed, a jolt of concern pushing through me. Why would Ashley's doctor be calling me this early? Was something wrong?

"Is Ashley okay?" I asked.

"I was calling to ask you the same thing. I wanted to check on her. We have not fully cleared her to be released. So I wanted to encourage you to bring her back over here to run a few more tests."

"What do you mean?"

"We need to make sure there're no lingering upper-respiratory issues—"

"Yes, I get that. But what are you talking about? 'Bring her back'?"

"Ashley left the hospital. She's not with you?"

"What? When?"

"I don't know for sure. But she wasn't here when I arrived first thing this morning. I figured you came and got her. Was I mistaken?"

"Wait . . . Hold up a second . . ." I pulled my phone away from my ear, began searching my text messages. There were a lot of unread messages from friends and acquaintances. But nothing from Ashley. "Are you sure, Doc? Maybe she just went to the lobby for coffee or something."

"We checked around. Ashley is no longer at the hospital, unless she's hiding in a closet for some reason."

I was up and out of bed now, walking over to our bathroom. I flipped on the light switch. Ashley's bathroom counter was clean and tidy, just the way it had been last night when I went to bed. Same with the primary closet. I didn't notice anything different that told me she had come home.

"Luke?"

"Look, Doc, I'll be right over. We'll figure this out."

I hung up and immediately dialed Ashley's number. It went straight to voice mail. No ringing. That usually meant her phone was off. Had she turned it off? Or was it dead? I went back to the closet and pulled on some blue jeans, a T-shirt, and a gray hoodie. My mind was spinning. Why would Ashley have left the hospital without telling me? Where would she have even gone? Could she be out in the kitchen right now? Or upstairs with Joy?

I typed out a quick text to her.

Hey, call me ASAP. Please.

I hit Send. I waited to see if the little dots that said she was responding would appear. They did not. Again, maybe her phone was dead.

I hurried out of our bedroom, hoping to see lights on in the kitchen or the living room. But they were all off. I hit the stairs and traveled down the hallway toward Joy's bedroom. There were no lights on anywhere upstairs, either. I poked my head into Joy's room. Her Tinker Bell night-light was on in the corner, casting a pink-and-purple glow throughout the room. It was clear that Ashley was not in bed with her daughter. I would need to stir Joy awake and take her with me over to the hospital. But then I knew Ashley didn't want me to bring her up there. Maybe Ms. Marie was already awake. I knew our neighbor to be an early riser. I'd seen her out walking on days when I had to travel before sunrise. Sitting on the edge of Joy's bed, I reached over and turned on the lamp on her nightstand.

My heart nearly stopped. Joy was not in the bed.

I pulled her pink comforter all the way down. No Joy. I jumped up and turned on the hanging chandelier light. I looked on the other side of the bed and then in the closet. My stepdaughter was nowhere to be found in the bedroom. What the hell? Now my heart was racing.

I popped back into the hallway, yelled, "Joy!"

No response. I yelled again. "Joy, where are you?"

Still nothing. I moved to the other upstairs bedrooms, flipping on every light. No sign of her. I went to the end of the hallway and checked inside Ashley's art studio. Joy wasn't in there, either. I kept yelling her name but getting no response. The house had never felt quieter. Where was my stepdaughter? I rushed back downstairs and searched every room in the house. Nothing. I thought of the indoor lap pool; a horrific image of a little girl floating in the water suddenly flashed through my mind. Could Joy have gotten into the water for some reason? She was a good little swimmer already, but you never knew. I hurried into the fully enclosed back-patio space. The door to the pool was still locked. I had put a digital keypad on it to keep this very thing from happening. I unlocked the door, flipped on the light, and felt a small measure of relief. She was not in the pool.

But then, where was she?

I ran back through the house and checked the garage. She was not in there, and the garage doors were both closed. I paused in the mudroom and stared at the security keypad. The alarm was not currently armed. I felt sure I'd set it last night. It was habit. One of the last things I always did before going to bed. I'd get a drink of water in the kitchen, go into the mudroom, set the alarm, and then head to the bedroom. I racked my brain.

Had I not set it last night?

Had I been thrown off by Ashley being in the hospital?

I thought about the security cameras. We had one camera by the front door and one over the garage. After opening the security app on my phone, I began scrolling backward through the night's stored video to see if anything popped up. But there was no sign of anyone entering our house from the front or the garage. I again thought about Ashley.

Could she have come home and taken Joy? Ashley had the security code to disarm the alarm. She could've even used her house key to come in the back door. But why would she do that? Why would she sneak into her own house from the back and grab her daughter without telling me? It didn't make any sense.

Still, I hoped it was true. The thought of someone else having taken Joy sent a wave of terror straight through me.

Something popped into my head that I thought might give me better insight into what had happened. I rushed back upstairs and returned to Joy's bedroom. I was looking for her favorite stuffed animal, a worn-out white rabbit she called Floppy. She'd gotten it when she was born and slept with it every night. She rarely went anywhere without it. There had been times I'd driven all the way back home to get it when we were out and Joy suddenly realized she did not have Floppy with her. I pulled all the covers off the bed—no sign of the stuffed animal anywhere. I went to the corner of the room, where built-in shelves held dozens of other stuffed animals. I began pulling them all out but still didn't find Floppy. I looked under the bed, in her bathroom and the closet. Floppy was gone. And I knew for certain Joy had had the stuffed animal in bed with her last night. If someone random had grabbed her from bed and bolted during the night, I doubted they would've made sure to take the stuffed rabbit. Perhaps Joy could've already had it tightly clutched in her arms, but I also found that unlikely. The child had crawled into bed with us many times. She was constantly moving around in her sleep, arms twisting, legs kicking.

I stood there a moment, baffled.

Ashley had to have taken her.

FIVE

I decided not to call the police yet about Joy. If Ashley had indeed come home to get her—which I suspected, even though it made zero sense—there was no reason to get the police involved. What would I say, anyway? *My stepdaughter is missing this morning, but her mother probably came home to get her without telling me.* I'd sound like an idiot. I needed to do some more searching before I took drastic action. I tried to track Ashley's phone through my own phone's Find My app, but no GPS signal popped up. Her phone had to be powered off. Was that intentional?

I left the house, then drove swiftly over to the hospital and parked in a loading zone right up front. I was trying not to let my mind go crazy, but I could feel an anxiety attack brewing. I needed to hold it off somehow. This would all likely be resolved in some logical way this morning. No need to go into a dark tailspin. After Jill had been killed, I'd begun having the attacks regularly. It would usually start with an anxious swirling in my stomach that would move to my chest and eventually make it hard for me to breathe. They would come out of nowhere, tiny triggers that sent me down a path where I felt like I was having a heart attack. I'd have to find a dark room somewhere, lie down, close my eyes, and breathe very slowly until it finally subsided. I squeezed my eyes shut and took several deep breaths now, letting each of them out as slowly as possible. It was working. I could feel myself starting to calm down.

My anxiety attacks had stopped altogether the day I met Ashley. And I'd only met Ashley because of Floppy, the stuffed bunny.

I studied the unique metal sculpture of three boys sitting together on a bench. One was reading a book, another was looking through binoculars, and the third was eating what looked like a sandwich. The sculpture was life-size and had probably been created to put in someone's garden. It was not my taste, but it was impressive. And so was the price tag: $12,000. But I had no doubt some wealthy individual was going to snatch it up.

It was a beautiful summer day, and hundreds of people, like me, were wandering about the fifty or so tent-covered booths at the annual Outdoor Arts Festival. I wasn't looking for any particular type of art; I just wanted to enjoy the festivities. It was my first full summer in Vail, and it was spectacular. The various squares were lined with the most colorful flowers I'd ever seen, which seemed to make people happy—except for one little girl I spotted across the way. She looked sad, sitting cross-legged under a tent, tears in her eyes. She was probably only two years old. Beside her, a young woman was painting with her back to me.

I walked over, knelt in the front of the girl. "Now that's the saddest face I may have ever seen."

The little girl looked at me, her bottom lip bulging out. "I can't find Floppy."

"Oh no. Who is Floppy?"

"It's her stuffed animal," the painter answered, sighing.

I looked up. The woman had dark, curly hair pulled up into a bunch on top of her head. There were little smudges of different-colored paints on her face. She wore denim overalls that were also covered in paint. She was a mess. But she was beautiful. She couldn't have been more than midtwenties, but her penetrating green eyes told me she'd already lived a lot of life.

"Unfortunately," the woman continued, "I can't leave my booth right now and go help her look. So we're not a happy camper."

"Maybe I can help."

The girl's face lit up. "Really?"

"That's very nice of you, sir, but unnecessary," the painter said. "I'm sure you didn't come here to the festival to search for a stuffed animal."

"Well, that may be true, but I'm not going to be able to enjoy myself now until I can help turn that frown upside down." I looked back at the girl. "What does Floppy look like?"

"She's a bunny."

"Okay. What color?"

"White."

"Where was the last time you remember having Floppy?"

The little girl pointed over my shoulder. "By the flowers."

I turned around and spotted a cart loaded with flowers across the street path. "Okay, I'll start there."

The painter chimed back in. "Sir, you really don't have to do this. I'm sure it will turn up eventually."

"Please, please," begged the little girl.

I smiled at the painter. "How can I say no to that?"

She gave me a small grin back with a head tilt and a slight eye twinkle that felt inviting to me. I really liked it.

I winked at the girl. "Wish me luck."

She beamed. "Good luck!"

I started by searching around the flower cart where the little girl had pointed. But there was no sign of a stuffed animal. So I began to branch out from there, circling through the other artists' tents and booths, making my way up and down the paver street surrounded by retail shops. After fifteen minutes, I began to lose hope. No sign of a stuffed animal anywhere. I thought about going into a toy shop and buying the little girl a new one. I hated the thought of returning to her with nothing. But then I spotted what had to be Floppy sitting in a metal chair right outside Rimini Gelato & Chocolate. The woman and the girl must've stopped by for a treat before heading over to her art tent.

I snagged the stuffed animal and headed back. I hid Floppy behind me with one hand as I approached the little girl again and put on my own pretend sad face. This made her bottom lip quiver. So I quickly pulled the bunny out and showed it to her.

Her eyes lit up like fireworks. "Floppy!"

She jumped up, grabbed her precious stuffed animal, and squeezed it tightly in both arms.

"You just made our day," the painter said to me.

"Mine, too. Look at the joy on her face."

"That's actually her name. Joy."

"Well, it fits perfectly."

"Say thank you, Joy," the painter instructed.

She hugged my leg. "Thank you!"

"My pleasure." I patted her on the head. "I'm Luke," I said to the painter, not wanting to leave just yet.

"Ashley."

I took in several of the paintings she had put out in her booth. They were all beautiful landscapes. Mountains, lakes, rivers, and gardens.

"These are fantastic, Ashley."

"Thank you. I should probably give you one for free. I would've had a miserable daughter for weeks, maybe months, if you'd not found Floppy. That's worth way more than one of my paintings."

"I highly doubt that." I paused. "How about an art lesson instead?"

I just threw it out there, took a chance. I had not asked anyone out since Jill died. I didn't think I was ready. But there was something about talking to Ashley. I couldn't put my finger on it. A freedom I felt inside. Like I was out of my own head for a moment. And I wanted to find out why I was feeling this way.

She paused, gave me a half smile. "I'm sorry, but I don't give lessons."

The pause was enough to give me hope, so I pushed forward. "I could be your first client. You never know where that could lead."

Another pause as she tried to figure me out.

"Mommy! Lesson, lesson!" Joy blurted out.

I smiled at Joy, turned back to Ashley. "What do you say? Just one short lesson. I've always wanted to paint. I just don't know where to start."

There was some truth to that. I'd always thought it would be healthy for me to find a creative outlet to balance out my work life. But I'd never pursued anything.

She pointed across the way. "There is a paint-by-numbers kit you can buy in the Market over there."

"Ouch," I replied. "Is that prejudgment on my talent level?"

She laughed. "If you're being serious, there are free classes at the library every week. Taught by great artists who can actually talk about what they're doing and why. I just go by feel. I don't really know how to teach feel."

"I've always been a feeler myself."

She gave me a small but suspicious grin. I had clearly shown my cards.

"We could do it right here," I suggested. "After the festival wraps up in a few hours."

Joy was cheering me on again.

"One lesson," Ashley said, but I saw that inviting eye twinkle again.

I was on another search for Floppy this morning. I got out of my car and entered the hospital. There was a different receptionist manning the main lobby desk. I mentioned who I was and asked to see Dr. Longview. He came out from the back hallway a few minutes later and met me in the quiet lobby. There was minimal activity on the ground floor at the moment.

"You still have not heard from her?" he asked.

I shook my head. "Does anyone here know *anything*?"

"I did more digging after speaking with you. From what I could gather, Ashley left the hospital unannounced around two this morning. No one saw her leave, but the nurse on duty said she was here one moment and then gone the next time she came by on her rotation.

The nurse called both Ashley's phone and your phone and left voice mails. She then reported it to our security officer, who did some more checking around but also couldn't find her. So the nurse logged it into our system as AMA."

"What is AMA?"

"Left against medical advice."

I hadn't bothered to listen to my voice mails this morning, so I didn't realize the nurse had called me during the night. I could feel my heart racing. Talking to the doctor had not squelched any of my fears. It had only poured fuel on the fire.

"My wife didn't say anything to anyone?" I asked.

"No, I don't believe so. She just left, I guess."

"It doesn't make sense. In the middle of the night?"

"I agree. I thought the timing was odd, even when I suspected you came here and picked her up without officially checking out."

"Do you have security cameras?"

"Of course. Everywhere but inside the private rooms."

"Can I view the footage?"

The doctor cocked his head. "Well, that's not something we usually do, Luke. We have privacy policies and federal regulations—"

"I get that, Doc, but my wife walked out of this hospital without telling anyone—including me, her husband. And on top of that, my stepdaughter was missing from our home this morning when I went into her bedroom. So I'm really freaking out here, okay? I'd like to see this with my own eyes."

"Your stepdaughter is missing?"

"Well, I don't know that for sure. I'm trying to figure this all out."

"Yeah, all right. Let me call our security guy."

Moments later, I was inside a security room, staring at multiple screens while a security officer brought up the digital footage. Dr. Longview was standing beside me, probably curious himself now as to what had happened.

"You said around two this morning?" the officer asked.

"Yes," the doctor said. "Between two and two twenty, I think."

The security officer punched on his keyboard. "Here we go. This is the hallway right outside her hospital room at 2:07."

I leaned in closer to one screen and watched as Ashley suddenly poked her head outside her room. She didn't immediately step into the hallway. It was like she was looking for something—or someone. She searched both ways and then crept out into the hallway. Ashley was still in her hospital gown. She'd tossed her burned clothes at the hospital. I was supposed to be bringing her something to wear home today. She was holding her small purse in one hand. Again, she paused, her head pivoting in both directions down the hallway. She waited until there was no hospital staff in the vicinity, then took a left and began walking forward, slowly at first, her head on a swivel. A brisker walk brought her to the end of the hallway.

The security officer switched camera views to the opposite direction, which showed Ashley approaching. She then pushed through a door and exited. The security officer again switched camera views to the internal stairs. Ashley hustled down them, looking kind of frantic, and pushed through yet another door. It led to the parking garage below the building. I couldn't believe what I was watching. Ashley paused in the entry to the garage, again searching everywhere. What was she doing? Who was she looking for? It was like she didn't want to be discovered. She didn't want anyone knowing she was leaving. Why? A few seconds later, Ashley left the garage on foot through an exit to the street and was out of view of any cameras.

I stood there a moment, so confused. My wife had left the building in nothing but her thin hospital gown. Even in the summer, temperatures in Vail can drop below forty at night. She had to have been freezing.

So why had my wife done that?

And where was she right now?

SIX

I felt numb as I walked out of the hospital. I wasn't even sure what to do next. Ashley had left of her own free will, and I had no idea where she'd gone. Joy had to be with her. Could Ashley have walked all the way to our home? That was possible. Vail was a small, walkable town, and we didn't live too far from the hospital. But it was hard to envision my wife creeping barefoot through the well-lit streets of Vail in the middle of the night, wearing nothing but her hospital gown. And I also couldn't wrap my mind around the idea that my wife would sneak into our home to get Joy without telling me.

Which left me wondering what kind of mental or emotional shape my wife was in at the moment. She'd looked completely paranoid in the security videos. Could Ashley have endured some kind of head trauma from the fire rescue that was causing her to act irrationally? Could she be having an adverse reaction to her pain medication that was somehow making her delusional? The doctor had said both were possible but unlikely based off his thorough examination. That was my worst fear, that Ashley could do something to harm herself or Joy. I kept trying her phone number, but it continued to go straight to voice mail. No response to any of my numerous texts. I'd fired off an email to her earlier—an account that she rarely used except with clients—but had received nothing back on that, either.

I had no answers. Only questions. And growing concern.

My car was still parked in the loading zone where I'd left it. The sun was starting to rise on the day. Somehow that made me feel better. Ashley and Joy were not out there wandering around the community in the dark. I started to make a mental list of various spots where Ashley might have gone. Coffee shops, cafés, and parks. Most other places would still be closed this early. I decided if I couldn't find Ashley and Joy this morning, I would go to the police and seek their help. But I was still holding on to hope that this was all a big misunderstanding. That maybe I would go back home right now, and Ashley and Joy would be there in the kitchen, making breakfast. And we'd all have a good laugh.

As I got to the door to my car, someone approached me from behind.

"Mr. Driskell?"

I turned. He was a clean-cut Asian man, probably in his thirties, with short black hair and wearing a black sport coat, white shirt, and black slacks.

"Yes?"

He pulled out a wallet and flipped it open to show me an identification badge. "I'm Special Agent Chang with the FBI. I'm assisting in the investigation into the fire at the school building yesterday."

I tilted my head. "Why is the FBI involved?"

He took out a small notepad and pen. "Standard operating procedure, in cases where we suspect potential arson."

"You think someone intentionally set the fire?"

"There are some signs indicating the possibility."

"That's horrible."

"Yes, that's why we're investigating."

"Okay. What can I do for you?"

"I need to ask you some questions about your wife."

"Ashley?"

"Yes, she was one of the first people on the scene. She could offer us valuable information, depending on what all she saw."

"Have you spoken directly with her?"

"No, not yet. I just got on the case this morning. The receptionist inside told me you were the husband."

I wondered if he knew that Ashley had walked out of the hospital during the middle of the night. Was that why he was talking to me? I had no desire to get into that conversation with him right now. That would likely make things more complicated for me, and I just wanted to get on with my search already.

"I honestly don't know very much," I explained. "Ashley and I haven't really talked in detail about what all happened yesterday. She's kind of traumatized."

"I've seen the video. That was an incredibly brave thing she did."

I nodded. "It was."

"Is she doing okay?"

I wasn't sure how to answer that. So I stuck to the facts. "A few burns that will take some time to heal. But she should be fine."

"Good. How long have you two been married?"

"Not long. Three months."

"Newlyweds? Congratulations."

"Thank you."

"Where did you guys meet?"

"Here in Vail."

"Ashley is a painter, right?"

"Yes."

"How about yourself?"

I furrowed my brow.

"We like to put together full profiles on all our interviewees," Chang explained. "Helps us better see the whole picture."

"I see. I'm part owner of a software company in Palo Alto."

"I grew up in San Francisco. Used to date a girl who worked for Apple, so I was in Palo Alto all the time. But you don't sound Californian."

"That's because I'm originally from Texas."

"I thought I recognized the accent. I worked in the Houston office for a while. What about Ashley? Where is she from?"

"Virginia." I was growing weary of the questions. The clock was ticking. I needed to find Ashley and Joy. "Look, Agent Chang, I don't mean to be rude, but I really need to get going."

"Just a couple more quick questions. The little girl, Joy. She is your stepdaughter?"

"Yes."

"Where is her real father?"

"He died before she was born."

"How tragic. Does your stepdaughter attend the school that caught on fire?"

"No."

"Then why was Ashley at the school yesterday?"

"I don't know." I pitched my head. "Wait, you don't think—"

"We have to investigate every possibility, Mr. Driskell." The FBI agent closed his notepad, stuffed it back into his jacket. "That's all for now. I appreciate your time."

As I watched the agent walk away and into the hospital, I suddenly felt very concerned. Would Ashley's odd disappearing act last night make her seem like an actual suspect? And how was Agent Chang going to react in a few minutes, when he found out Ashley was no longer in the building, and I hadn't mentioned anything about it?

I had to find her before this turned into an even bigger ordeal.

SEVEN

I drove straight from the hospital over to the day-care facility where Ashley had saved those kids. I wondered if there was any chance she could have walked there last night and retrieved her car. But as soon as I pulled up to the property, I noticed her Mazda SUV still sitting along a curb beside the school. I took in the destroyed building. Part of the brick had crumbled on one end. The same end where Ashley had been inside. The rest of the facility was charred and black. It was going to need a major restoration. Or they might have to tear the whole thing down. I thought about what the FBI agent had said earlier. Could someone have intentionally set the building on fire? Who would do that with children inside?

I parked directly behind Ashley's car, got out, walked over. The doors were all locked. I didn't have an extra set of keys on me. They were hanging on a hook in our mudroom back home. I glanced inside all the car windows. Joy's car seat was strapped in the back. There was a pile of Barbie dolls in the seat next to it, Cheerios in the cracks. Ashley had a canvas bag of paint supplies in the front passenger seat. I could see her familiar travel coffee mug in the cup holder. It was white, with Vail, Colorado scrolled across it in gold. This made me smile for a moment. Ashley had purchased it on our first date while we were out shopping. I'd offered to buy it for her as a gift, but she wouldn't let me. I thought about that first evening together. She hadn't allowed me to spend much money on her at all. Which had turned out to be the best thing for us.

It had been six weeks since we'd met at the arts festival, where Ashley had reluctantly agreed to give me the art lesson. We'd laughed a lot that day, and she really seemed to enjoy spending the time with me. When I asked her out on an actual date at the end, to my dismay, she declined. I had been sure there was a mutual spark between us, so I felt confused by it.

At first, I tried to move on. I felt guilty about having such a strong pull toward another woman so soon after Jill had died. But I couldn't get Ashley off my mind. So for the next six weeks, I showed up at every one of her art-gallery exhibits. I would openly flirt, she'd laugh me off, and we'd have light and fun little exchanges in between her greeting other gallery guests. I would then hang around until the shows were over and ask her out again. Coffee, lunch, breakfast, dinner, a walk—anything. I faced repeated rejection, Ashley always saying she just didn't feel like it was the right time for her to start seeing anyone. She needed to focus on Joy. At one point, I specifically asked if she'd prefer I not show up at any more of her exhibits. But she dismissed that offer and said she enjoyed having me around her shows. I made her laugh. It was maddening. I knew we had something strong between us. But she would just shut down when I wanted to take things a step further. Why? I could see real tension in her eyes. An internal struggle. A woman who wanted to spend time with me, but something was holding her back.

I kept showing up anyway. Each time, I would see her immediately flash a smile, though she would play it off and pretend to be annoyed.

"You again?" she'd say, rolling her eyes.

"Me, again," I'd say, matching her eye rolls with my most charming smile.

I broke through on my fifth attempt. I was helping her pack up her things in her car after one exhibit. I almost felt stupid saying it, but I did it anyway.

"I don't suppose—"

She cut me off. "Dinner would be nice."

My mouth dropped open. "Really?"

She laughed. "It might be the only way for me to finally get rid of you."

With my one shot, I was determined to impress her that night. So I made reservations at a fancy restaurant called Montauk, a fine-dining steak-and-seafood establishment where I could easily drop five hundred bucks, especially if we dipped into the caviar menu. I picked Ashley up in Eagle, thirty miles up the road, and drove her back over to Vail. I was excited. But she seemed very reserved. Maybe she was just nervous. I had to carry most of the conversation. Things seemed free and easy between us while at the art exhibits, but maybe that was because we'd only been shooting the breeze—we weren't talking about our real lives. Ashley seemed pretty closed down about her life, except when talking about Joy. So I mostly camped out there. I didn't want to push her and screw this up.

After parking, we walked into the restaurant and checked our jackets at the front. Ashley looked especially beautiful in a black cocktail dress and heels, her long dark, curly hair falling over her shoulders. She even wore a touch more makeup than usual, which she didn't need. I was so used to seeing her in overalls, T-shirts, tennis shoes, her hair always a painted mess. She looked great like that to me, but she was a real stunner that night. We were seated at a private and romantic table I'd requested by the windows. Everything was perfect. Or so I thought.

"What do you think?" I asked her.

I knew she'd never been there before from our discussion earlier.

She looked around, shrugged. "It's okay, I guess."

She grinned. I laughed.

"This is how you try to impress all of your dates?" she asked.

Ashley had the playful eye roll thing down pat.

"Just you. I haven't been on a date in a while."

"Come on, I don't buy that. Mary at the International Gallery calls you Vail's most eligible bachelor. Tall, dark, and handsome."

"You think I'm handsome?"

She gave me a coy smile. "Mary's words, not mine."

I laughed but then felt a check inside. Ashley wasn't the only one being reserved about sharing private information. I had not yet mentioned anything to her about Jill. I think I was afraid of her reaction when I told her the truth about how my wife and unborn child had died. Maybe she already knew. Most people immediately google anyone of interest. But I didn't want to do or say anything that might chase her away.

A waiter came by, handed us menus, and took our drink orders. When Ashley opened her menu, she nearly gasped. Then put her hand to her mouth, embarrassed.

"What's wrong?" I asked.

"Have you seen these prices?"

"Well, yes, I've been here many times."

She leaned forward, whispered, "I can't eat here, Luke."

"Why?"

"You cannot spend this kind of money on me."

I couldn't tell if she was joking or not. Was this a game?

"Ashley, it's fine. Trust me, I can easily afford it."

Her wide eyes were back on the menu. "I just . . . Do people really spend three hundred dollars on caviar?"

"Yes, some do."

She continued to whisper, as if she were afraid of offending the waitstaff or other guests at surrounding tables. "Do you know how many homeless people I could feed at that price?"

She was being serious. "Uh, I'm guessing quite a few."

"Probably fifty."

I wasn't sure of my next move. "Do you want to leave?"

She gave me a sympathetic head tilt, considered her words. "Look, I really do appreciate this, Luke. Please don't take it the wrong way. I don't mean to imply that there is something wrong about any of this. There is certainly a time and place for a meal in a fabulous restaurant like this one.

But, honestly, it's just not me. It never will be. If you want to impress me, let's take the expected price of this meal, donate it to the homeless ministry where I volunteer, and instead go eat cheap, greasy cheeseburgers at some hole-in-the-wall joint." She briefly paused but then continued before I could say anything. "I will also understand if you just want to call it a night. I'm sure this is not what you expected. I'm sorry."

I stared at her a moment, feeling something happening in my chest. Like a pressure-release valve being flipped open and the air bursting out. For so long, my self-worth had been directly tied to my overall financial success. It played into everything: The clothes I wore. The car I drove. The women I dated. While I loved Jill, I knew for certain she would've never been interested in me if I hadn't already achieved a certain stature in life. I'd been okay with that for a while. But I'd always felt the pressure to keep my place at that table. It felt so freeing to sit there with someone who placed so little value in that. Ashley had already made it clear that if we were going to have any future together, it would have to be with the real me. I smiled so wide I could feel the tension near my ears.

"Don't be sorry. I hate caviar anyway. Let's get the hell out of here right now and go find a good burger. I know just the place."

Fifteen minutes later, we were sitting in a booth with cheeseburgers, fries, and milkshakes on the table in front of us and a jukebox in the corner playing old country songs. Although Ashley seemed much more relaxed, she was still so reserved about sharing her past. But that didn't keep me from trying.

"Where did you grow up?" I asked, stuffing a fry into my mouth.

"Virginia."

"I've been to Virginia once, about three years ago. Had a client in Richmond. Only spent a day there, but it seemed like a nice place. You still have family there?"

"No, I don't."

"They move away?"

She broke eye contact and stared down at her burger. "I don't really have any family."

I leaned in to the table. "No one?"

"No, I was raised in foster care. Never knew my parents. No siblings. Nobody."

"That must have been hard."

She was still staring at her food. "It was. And if it's okay with you, I don't really want to talk about it."

"Of course that's okay."

It now made more sense to me why she was so guarded with her past. There was clearly a lot of pain there. We had a moment of awkward silence, so I decided to fill it with my own vulnerability. Something I was not prone to do with anyone. But the sad look in Ashley's eyes at that moment compelled me to swallow my own pride.

"I didn't know my parents, either."

She looked up at me.

"They died when I was four," I continued. "So I don't really remember much of anything about them."

"I'm sorry, Luke."

"I just wanted you to know that I get it. I understand. At least a little. I still had my grandfather around."

"He raised you?"

"Yes, sort of. Kind of raised myself. Pop mostly sat around in his recliner all day, drinking. Although we had a few good moments."

"Like what?"

"Well, I was a scrawny kid growing up. This got me picked on a lot. Pop saw me come home with a black eye one day when I was eleven and decided he wanted to teach me how to box to defend myself. He'd boxed when he was in the marines. He found some gloves in a metal case in the old barn next to our trailer and strapped them on me. It was probably the best two weeks of my entire childhood. We spent every day together after school, learning the sport. Pop was firm but playful. He had to box with one arm, because he'd lost the other in a trucking accident. He really took training me seriously, like he'd finally found some pride in being able to help raise

me up in the world. But Pop eventually got bored and tired and went back to his drinking. And that was that."

Ashley picked at her fries. "I had a foster dad like that for a little while. Drank a lot. Didn't really engage with us foster kids very much. Until he found me trying to shoot a basketball through a hoop in the driveway. I was eight and could barely throw it high enough. But he liked basketball a lot, so he started showing me the proper form. For the next week, he would take me out to the driveway after he got home from work and shoot hoops with me. But then I got yanked out of there by CPS."

"Why?"

Her face went dark. "He had a bad side. He, uh, did some things . . ."

She paused, swallowed. I could tell by the look in her eyes that sharing this was hitting her hard. I wanted to protect her from it, so I jumped in.

"Funny you mention basketball, because it basically saved my life."

"Really?"

"Yeah. After I learned to box, I started fighting back at school. Bullies began leaving me alone once they'd taken enough of my blows. But I got suspended regularly and labeled a troublemaker by teachers. Things were looking kind of bleak for me for a while, until I sprouted my freshman year in high school. I grew six inches to my current six foot two, which got me noticed by the basketball coach. He'd spotted me out playing some hoops at a friend's house one afternoon and wanted me to try out for the team. Basketball quickly became my escape. I worked hard at it. Coach even brought a portable hoop over to my trailer and set it up in the dirt near the barn. I spent hundreds of hours out there. By the time I was a junior, I was the starting point guard on varsity and began to get some interest from smaller colleges. Because an athletic scholarship was the only chance a poor kid like me had at going to college—which I knew I needed to do to somehow make money—I would stay up until midnight every night working on my game. Pop would even play HORSE *with me. He had a decent one-arm set shot. And he started coming to my games and cheering. Sometimes a little too drunkenly loud and would get some stares."*

She kind of laughed at that. "Did you get a scholarship?"

"I did. To Rice University in Houston. Pop was so proud. We celebrated by going to his favorite barbecue-and-beer joint. He bought a round of beers for all his buddies there and then made a grand toast to me: 'To my grandson, Luke, the best damn kid around.'"

She smiled. "That's a great story, Luke."

"It was. Until Pop died in his sleep that night."

"Are you joking?" she asked.

"I'm afraid not."

I swallowed, took a moment. Thinking about it always got me choked up. Pop had still had a smile on his face when I walked into his bedroom the next morning and tried to stir him. But he was gone. And so was any remnant of family.

"I'm sorry. That must have been devastating."

"It was. So I've been on my own, like you, for most of my life."

"I know that's a really difficult thing."

"Maybe that's why we're here, Ashley. You and I have scars most people will never be able to understand. And that connects us."

"Maybe," she said.

We both took a long moment, staring at each other, before Ashley seemed to get uncomfortable with it and changed directions.

"Well, it obviously hasn't held you back. You've gone on to do wonderful things."

"I made the most of the college opportunity. While I never became a star in college, I was a solid role player. But I really dug into my academics and pursued a degree in computer science. I'd dabbled a lot with computers in high school, mainly because I was too broke to ever buy a new laptop and had to always figure out how to upgrade my own. I graduated with honors. A teammate's father offered me a job at his software company in Palo Alto, so I packed my bags at graduation and moved to Northern California. For five years, I worked my tail off on a team led by two senior associates on all kinds of cool projects. I basically slept at the office every night and became

invaluable to them and the firm. When the two senior associates decided to go out on their own, they begged me to go with them. They called me a rising star. I was hesitant at first, out of loyalty to the man who gave me my first job. But then they offered me equal partnership in their new company. I oversaw new product development. We hit it big on several product launches right out of the gate. Wealthy investors started flocking to us. And then we went public. The rest, as they say, is history."

"Wow. You're an inspiration."

"Thanks, I guess."

She wrinkled her brow. "That didn't sound too enthusiastic."

I sighed. "You know, money is great and all—"

"But it's not everything," she said, correctly finishing my thought.

"That's becoming clearer to me every day."

She reached across the table, squeezed my hand.

"Thanks for sharing, Luke."

In my gut, I think I knew that night I would marry Ashley. I got back in my Range Rover and drove straight home. I prayed I would find Ashley and Joy waiting for me there. I kept expecting them to just be somewhere obvious. That was the only thing that made sense to me. But the house was the same as when I'd left it earlier that morning.

I made a quick path to the primary closet. I wanted to take a closer look at Ashley's side to see if I could tell whether she'd been there during the night. I was a heavy sleeper. Ashley would usually have to shove me hard to wake me up if she needed something during the night. She could've very easily crept into the closet without waking me, ditched the hospital gown, and grabbed a new set of clothes. I examined everything again. All the drawers of her tall built-in dresser were closed. There were no clothes lying around on the hardwood floor. No hospital gown in the laundry basket. I saw nothing that pushed me in one direction or the other.

I left the house in my car and pulled into Ms. Marie's driveway. I just wanted to be sure that Ashley had not dropped Joy there for some reason. Again, I had no idea what kind of mental place my wife had been in. Ashley could've somehow subconsciously defaulted to a normal day. Ms. Marie answered the door in a fluffy white robe. Because the house was quiet, I immediately knew my stepdaughter was not there.

"Good morning, Luke," she said. "Is everything okay?"

She must've noticed the concerned look on my face. I tried to play it off. "Oh, yes, all is good. Have you seen Ashley this morning, by any chance?"

"I have not. But I heard all about what happened yesterday. So amazing—I'm just shocked. Is she doing okay?"

I figured Ms. Marie would know about yesterday's events by now. "Yes, she's going to be just fine. Thank God. Sorry I didn't mention it yesterday when picking up Joy. Ashley didn't want her to know what happened. She thought it might scare Joy. Anyway, we've had some miscommunication this morning about our plans, so I thought I'd stop by to check with you."

"I see. Well, I haven't heard from her. But I will be here all day. Please don't hesitate if you need me for anything at all."

"Thank you, Ms. Marie."

From there, I drove straight over to Vail Village. I took a moment to pull up my American Express account on my phone. Ashley only used one of my credit cards. She didn't want a card in her own name. She told me she'd screwed up with credit cards back in college and it had ruined her credit. She never wanted to go through that stressful experience again, even if we could easily pay the bill each month. There were no new charges listed on my account this morning. She hadn't used the card. But she could be using cash. That's how she'd paid for everything when we first met.

I knew Ashley to frequent several of the local coffee shops. She enjoyed sipping chai lattes and drawing sketches on her pad for possible future paintings. I would often join her with my laptop. I stopped by Yeti's Grind first. I didn't see her anywhere in the outdoor-seating area, so I went inside. She was not in there, either. I thought how odd it would be to walk into a coffee shop and see her simply sitting there, enjoying coffee, Joy scribbling in a coloring book, as if everything were fine. But that's what I hoped would happen. Then Ashley would explain to me that she had just needed a private moment with her daughter. Or maybe yesterday's event somehow had pushed her to take some alone time to evaluate her life. I was grasping at straws.

I asked one of the familiar baristas—a girl with purple streaks in her hair and several nose rings—if she'd seen Ashley this morning. She told me no, but she'd seen the rescue video and thought it was so cool. I walked over to Unravel Coffee next. They had not seen her. No sign of Ashley or Joy anywhere. I crossed the village to Two Arrows Coffee. Same result. No Ashley. No Joy. No one had seen them this morning. But *everyone* had watched yesterday's video. I could tell a lot of them were confused why her husband had questions about her possibly being in their coffee shops. I casually played off each exchange as a simple miscommunication with my wife.

I drove over to the community church, where we attended on Sundays. I hadn't been a regular churchgoer before I met Ashley. But she was devoted. She taught Joy's Sunday school class every week. And she would often come over during weekdays to spend time in the small chapel, which was left open for prayer during the day. The small parking lot was nearly empty. I entered through the main chapel doors, began easing down the center aisle. I spotted only two people near the front, sitting in pews, heads bowed. Neither of them was Ashley. I did a full circle through the chapel and then left.

My desperation was growing.

Where the hell was she? And why had she taken Joy?

I thought of another breakfast spot where my wife liked to take Joy for special Mommy-daughter dates: Vintage, a French brasserie–style restaurant with terrific beignets. Joy would usually get her whole face covered in white sugar powder. I made the trek across the paver streets of the village. Vintage was always packed, and I could see people sitting at outside tables and more inside at windows. The mimosas and Bloody Marys were flowing. I didn't see my wife or stepdaughter at any of the tables. The entrance was tucked back in a short alleyway, so I headed in that direction.

Stepping inside, I asked the young hostess about Ashley, even showed her a photo on my phone. But she hadn't seen her, either. I was losing hope that I would find Ashley simply hanging out at a coffeehouse or breakfast place this morning. Something else had to be going on. That made my stomach turn because I had no idea what it could be. I was staring down at my phone as I left the restaurant, trying to locate other spots where I might find Ashley on a map of the town, when something caught my attention out of the corner of my eye. I looked up toward the end of the alley, near the street, and felt certain I saw Ashley's face poking around the corner, looking straight at me. It was only a split second, and then she was gone.

My heart jumped. I sprinted forward and nearly knocked down a couple out walking as I skidded around them onto the sidewalk. I quickly apologized without ever looking at them, because I was so focused up ahead. I saw a few people coming and going on the same sidewalk. But no Ashley. I ran forward again, darting around the other people, searching both sides of the street, even pausing to look into the windows of parked cars along the curb.

This didn't make any sense. Where had she gone?

"Ashley!" I yelled.

This caused people to turn and stare at me. I didn't care. I spun around in a full circle, yelled her name again, searching in all directions. It had to have been her. I knew my wife. I knew that face, those eyes.

But she was nowhere to be found.

EIGHT

I couldn't process how real it had felt to see Ashley staring at me from a distance one moment and then be completely gone the next. The more I thought about it, the less likely it seemed. Was I the one losing my mind now? Did I want to find her so much that I'd seen something that wasn't actually there? I had to admit it was possible. I'd been trying to will it into existence all morning. Sitting on a bench, I began calling people who knew both of us as a couple. I played the same casual card I had earlier with Ms. Marie and the coffee baristas—looking for Ashley, miscommunication, et cetera—but not even one of them had heard from her. However, they all wanted to talk about what had happened with the school fire and the kids. Everyone had seen the video. It felt so strange to be talking about my wife, the hero, considering my current circumstances. I did my best to placate them while also quickly getting off the phone.

I then continued my search around town for several more hours as other retail stores and popular venues began to open. I started with the most obvious places—the art galleries. But nobody from any of the local art galleries had seen or heard from her. Many of them had reached out by phone or text but had not heard back. I stepped inside every store where I knew Ashley had shopped or frequented. It seemed so stupid to be going into a women's clothing store and asking if they'd seen my wife, like she might have just been out shopping or something after fleeing the hospital last night. But what the hell else was I going to do? I also drove back and forth to our home several times throughout the morning, hoping with each return I might find my wife and stepdaughter there. These hopes were repeatedly dashed.

I was going crazy. And I felt helpless.

Early afternoon, I decided to expand my search and drove thirty miles up the road to the town of Eagle, where Ashley and Joy had been living when I'd first met them. Maybe they'd returned there for some reason. I needed to explore all possibilities. Eagle was less pretentious than Vail. It had much more of a blue collar–town feel. Mom-and-pop stores and family-owned restaurants. True locals. And more affordable living. I wasn't sure where to go to potentially find Ashley. We hadn't spent much time in Eagle during our courtship. So I wasn't familiar with her favorite local coffeehouses or hangouts. I drove slowly through historic downtown just to see if I might spot her anywhere. I even stopped at a few places and asked questions.

The only other place I could think to go was her former apartment complex. Ashley had lived in a tiny first-floor, one-bedroom apartment unit at a place called Castle Creek. The apartment bedroom probably wouldn't fit our current king-size bed. A kitchen and living area that was basically a shared space. While dating, we hadn't spent much time at her apartment, of course, and I hadn't been back over here since moving day. But I wondered if there was any chance Ashley and Joy could be at one of her former neighbors', even though I'd never heard her mention any of them.

I parked outside her building, got out, and found Ashley's former unit. I knocked on her door first. Maybe Ashley, in her confused state, had tried to return home here. Again, I was grasping at flimsy straws. A college-age guy in jeans and a white tank top answered the door. He had tattoos up both arms.

"Hey, sorry to bother you," I said. "My wife lived in your unit up until a few months ago. I know this sounds strange, but any chance you've seen this woman today?"

I held up my phone, which had a photo of Ashley on the screen.

He barely looked at it. He seemed high. "Nah, man. Ain't seen no one."

"You sure? No one has come by?"

"I dunno. I just woke up."

"All right, thanks."

He shut the door. I moved over to the unit on the left, but no one answered the door. I then knocked on the door to the right. This time someone did answer—a balding, elderly gentleman with wisps of white hair above both of his ears, wearing gray sweatpants and a Broncos jersey. The man immediately gave me the side-eye, like I might be there to solicit.

"Yes?" he grunted.

"Sorry to bother you, sir. My name is Luke Driskell. My wife, Ashley, and her daughter, Joy, used to live here next to you."

"Who? The painter?"

"Yes, correct."

"Odd duck. What do you want?"

Somehow I didn't think Ashley would've come to this apartment for shelter. "Strange question, I know, but have you seen her around here this morning?"

His face bunched up. "You lost your wife?"

"Not exactly. Just a miscommunication."

He kind of laughed at me. "My wife used to wander off in the mall. Took me damn near forever to find her sometimes. I hate the mall."

"Not my favorite place, either."

"No, I haven't seen her. She had a cute kid, though."

"Okay, thanks." I pivoted to leave but then turned back around before he closed the door. "Hey, why did you call Ashley an odd duck?"

He shrugged. "Don't mean nothing by it. Was just odd to hear a young gal like that praying in Chinese every night."

My eyes narrowed. "What are you talking about?"

He threw a thumb over his shoulder. "Our back patios are right next to each other. Separated by one very thin wall. I like to sit out there late at night, after Barbara goes to sleep, and sneak a cigarette or two. Maybe some whiskey. Your wife would often come out on her own patio. I could see her through a crack. She'd be holding a Bible and start quietly praying. I don't think she ever knew I was out here, because I always sat in the dark. I wasn't trying to invade her privacy or anything. Hell, I could hardly understand a word she was saying other than the repeated use of 'Jesus.' But she'd sometimes spend thirty minutes out there, just going on and on."

I wasn't sure what to think. I'd never heard Ashley speak a word of Chinese. Not even to Joy. So I pressed him on it.

"How do you know it was Chinese?" I asked.

"Served in the navy. Spent some time over there." He kind of laughed at me again. "Seems you don't know your wife too well. But, hell, I guess I'm still discovering things about Barbara, even after fifty years together. Women will always be a damn mystery to me."

NINE

I drove home pondering what the neighbor had told me. I guessed it wasn't out of the realm of possibility that Ashley could know some of the Chinese language. After all, I knew Joy's father had Chinese roots. But to spend thirty minutes praying in the language? Ashley would have to be fluent. Was that possible? If so, why would she keep it from me? I would find something like that to be fascinating and impressive. I knew business associates who were trying to learn the language for international networking. They all said it was hard as hell to pick up. I often found Ashley praying for long periods of time on our back deck, sometimes out loud—from the little I'd overheard, it was always in English. I wasn't sure what to believe. While the old neighbor was kind of goofy, he didn't seem senile. And considering he wasn't all that interested in talking to me in the first place, I had no reason to suspect he would make up something like that.

At the moment, it didn't matter. The only thing that mattered was finding Ashley and Joy. And I had failed so far in that regard. I checked my watch. Ashley had left the hospital at two in the morning. It was now nearing four in the afternoon. I couldn't believe she'd been gone for nearly fourteen hours without any communication with me. I couldn't recall another time since we'd been married when we'd gone more than a few hours without at least a quick text back and forth. It was just our nature. We were always checking in. We liked to be connected. So I had been walking around all day feeling like a piece of me was missing.

I couldn't do this on my own anymore. I had nowhere else to look and felt emotionally drained. I didn't want to keep pretending with everyone that everything was okay. I needed to go to the police. But I first wanted to make another quick trip home, just to check one more time—a Hail Mary of sorts. I parked in the center of our driveway instead of the garage since it was going to be a brief trip in and out of the house. I approached the glass front door, pulled out my house key. But when I went to stick the key in the slot, I noticed the door was unlocked. I paused. Had I not locked it the last time I was here? I turned the handle and pushed it open. I felt my heart start pumping with hope. Were they finally home?

Stepping inside, I immediately called out for her. "Ashley?"

No response.

I called again. "Ashley? Joy?"

Nothing. I felt my heart sink. I turned back to the front door. I guessed it was possible I'd left it unlocked the last time I'd popped in simply because my mind was all over the place. Sighing, I walked down the hallway toward the main suite because I needed to go to the bathroom. As I entered, I glanced to my left. The light was on in the closet. That made me stiffen. I *always* turned it off. Again, habit. I was a creature of habit. I felt certain I had not left the light on earlier.

I hesitantly stepped inside the closet. I examined Ashley's side first. It still seemed the exact same as earlier. Then I poked my head over on my side of the closet. That's when I cursed. We kept a nice set of luggage stored in the corner. One of the carry-on suitcases had been rolled out a few feet. I felt my heart begin to race again. Could it have been Ashley? Could she have come home while I was over in Eagle? I ran a hand through my hair, trying to think. Or had I moved it earlier? Was I losing my mind? Moving closer to the luggage, I began counting. All the pieces to the set were still there. If it was her, she hadn't taken any of the suitcases. But then I thought about the blue-and-pink duffel bag she always used when traveling overnight for art shows. She kept it right here with the luggage.

I pulled all the luggage out but didn't see her duffel bag anywhere. I hurried back over to her side and searched the shelves above her hanging clothes. No duffel bag. It was gone. What did that mean? Could Ashley have taken the bag? Was she planning to leave town? The thought of that sent a cold shiver straight through me. Could Ashley have possibly left me? To this point, I had not allowed myself to go down that kind of dark road. Was that what this was all about? I shook my head. There was no way. She had no reason. Our life was great together. We barely had arguments, much less any fighting. I doted on every single move she made. Even more so with Joy.

Still, I couldn't argue with the fact that her duffel bag was gone.

I grabbed my phone off the bathroom counter, began looking up local rental-car places, and started placing calls. Ashley couldn't have left town on foot. And she hadn't taken her car. I'd driven by the day-care facility several times today to make sure it was still parked there. I couldn't even believe my mind was going to such a place. My chest felt so tight I could barely breathe. Every time I got someone on the phone, I told them I was checking on a booking for my wife. Each rental-car place looked up her information. They all told me they had no such record—Ashley had not rented a car with them. I was unsure how she would even do it. I kept checking my American Express account, and there were still no charges listed for today. How would Ashley rent a car or even buy a bus ticket?

TEN

"This is what I know," I explained to my friends. "Ashley walked out of the hospital in the middle of the night last night. No word about it to anyone. Joy was gone when I got up this morning. Ashley's favorite duffel bag is missing from our closet. I haven't heard a single word from her all day today. No calls. No texts. No emails. As a matter of fact, her phone has been shut off all day, because no GPS signal ever pops up in my Find My app. I've searched everywhere I can think of for her but with no luck. I'm confused and completely distraught, which is why I came over here to see you guys."

I was sitting in a cushioned chair on the back patio of a fourth-floor apartment in the Solaris Residences, a luxury condo complex in the heart of Vail overlooking the main plaza—where they had ice-skating in the winter—with a spectacular view straight up Vail Mountain. Mark and Susan Banks owned the three-bedroom apartment. Ashley and I had become friends with them this past year. Susan had been an early fan of Ashley's art, and Mark was just a fun guy to be around. He owned several mattress stores throughout Colorado and spent most of his time snowboarding during the winter and mountain biking during the summer. We also golfed together. Susan loved art and yoga, which was why she connected so well with Ashley. By my estimation, Susan was probably Ashley's closest friend in town. Not that Ashley had too many close friends; she was a bit of a loner like me. This was probably why things felt so easy between us. We were just two introverts who mostly wanted to spend our free time at home together.

Mark handed me a beer, sat in the cushioned chair next to me. He was a big guy with broad shoulders—a former minor league baseball catcher—so the chair threatened to collapse every time he sat down. Susan was the opposite, petite with short blonde hair. She currently had a glass of white wine in her hand and was pacing around the patio. The sun was setting behind the mountains in front of us. A very long day was ending, and I still had no idea how to bring my family back together.

"I reached out a couple of times today," Susan mentioned. "I never heard back from Ashley. But I didn't think anything of it. Especially after you and I briefly talked this morning and you didn't mention anything. I figured she was at home resting and she'd call back when she felt up to it."

"You talk to the police?" Mark asked.

I nodded. "I just came from there, explained the situation. They said they'd start making some initial inquiries but felt the most logical conclusion was Joy was with her mother, who didn't want to be found at the moment. They said if nothing changes by tomorrow morning to let them know. And I guess they would put even more effort into it."

"Have you told anyone else she's missing?" Susan asked.

"Not yet. You're the first, other than the police. I didn't want to say anything to anyone, because I kept expecting to find Ashley and Joy. I didn't want to make it into a bigger issue unless it had to be. But now here I am, and I'm not sure what to do next."

"And you called all the galleries?" Susan asked.

"Yes. I visited each one in person. Nobody has seen or heard from her. Hell, I've been *everywhere* in this town, most places multiple times. Nothing. Ashley and Joy are just gone without any explanation."

I stared at the empty sofa in front of me. That's where Ashley always sat when we came over to have drinks on the patio and enjoy the view. We'd just been here a few days ago. Susan had made homemade pizza. The girls had sat on the sofa, talking about who was doing what in the local art scene, while Mark and I talked about baseball. It was surreal that Ashley wasn't here with me right now. And the conversation had turned so dramatically.

"Does Ashley have family nearby?" Mark asked.

"Just me. She grew up in foster care. There's no family anywhere."

"I didn't know that," Susan said.

"She doesn't like to talk about it."

"Yeah, she's private about a lot of things," Susan added. "'Course, it never bothers me too much. I talk enough for the both of us."

Mark leaned forward in his chair, elbows on the armrests. "Has Ashley said anything about wanting to go somewhere? Maybe a trip she wanted to take?"

"No, she doesn't like to travel. She's afraid of flying. She had a traumatic experience a couple years ago with extreme turbulence. So she always pushes back when I mention taking a vacation somewhere we can't drive. Plus, she doesn't want to be away from Joy for more than one night. That's why we didn't go on a real honeymoon. I wanted to take her to Fiji, but she talked me out of it. So we spent one night over in Aspen instead."

"Could she have driven somewhere?" Mark asked.

"Maybe. But she doesn't have her car. And I called every local rental-car place. They have no reservations under her name."

"This is so crazy, Luke." Susan sighed. "I mean, she's the talk of the town today, but in such a good way. What she did yesterday was incredible. So it's hard to believe we're even having this conversation right now."

"Believe me, I know. It doesn't feel real."

"She can't be thinking rationally," Mark said.

"That's my fear. That something happened to her when she rescued those kids. Like she banged her head hard and got a severe concussion, or something traumatic like that, which is causing her to not be in her right mind. Because I can't explain any of this. Nothing makes sense. And I'm afraid she might do something to hurt herself or to even harm Joy."

"She would never harm Joy," Susan asserted.

"Not when she's in her right mind," I agreed. "But if she's not thinking straight or is confused or paranoid, you never know. All these crazy scenarios have been building up in my head all day."

"How can we help?" Mark asked. "We'll do anything. I'll print up a thousand flyers and hang them all over town. I'll call everyone I know. I'll shut my stores down and bring all my employees here if we want to put together some kind of search crew. Whatever it takes."

"You don't need to do that."

"We've got to get the word out, buddy. We can't just sit around and hope that she walks through the door. If she's unstable, we need to find her ASAP. Maybe not flyers, but we need to do something."

"You're right." It felt good to hear someone say that, to have someone jumping into this foxhole with me. Carrying this around all day by myself had pushed my nerves to the limit, and inviting Mark and Susan inside this nightmare with me brought some much-needed relief. "I think I have an idea."

"To get the word out around town?" Mark asked.

"Maybe the whole state. I need to make a phone call."

ELEVEN

I got up at four o'clock the next morning to make the two-hour drive into Denver, which was not a problem for me. I hadn't slept a wink all night anyway. How could I with everything swirling through my head? Plus, every time I heard the slightest noise in the house, I'd pop straight out of bed and go looking, hoping, praying, begging God to let it be Ashley and Joy so this nightmare would finally be over. But the nightmare continued. I held on to some hope that my efforts this morning would change that. I'd gotten several voice mails yesterday from various TV news producers, both local and national, who were all wanting to get the story about my hero wife. I had called one of them back last night, a producer for *Good Morning, Denver*, a news-and-variety show that was broadcast throughout Colorado. Ashley and I often had the show on the TV in our bathroom in the morning while we were getting ready for our day. She liked the two hosts.

It was hard for me to leave Vail. There was a pull to remain local in case Ashley finally showed up. But I couldn't just make the same rounds today as I had yesterday, hoping something would change. I needed to be proactive. I arrived at the TV building in Denver around six. It was still dark outside. A young clerk with bushy brown hair met me in the lobby and guided me through hallways deeper into the building. We stopped in front of a glass wall that showcased the TV studio on the other side. I could see the familiar hosts up on a small, well-lit stage. There was a group of crew members in the dark, behind camera gear and computers.

"You can wait here," the clerk said. "I'll go get Mr. Pederson."

I stood there, waiting by myself, watching the show happening in front of me, feeling incredibly anxious. My fingers were shaking. Not because I was nervous to talk in front of people. I'd done this a lot in the tech world. But not with these kinds of circumstances. Not when I knew Ashley would absolutely hate what I was about to do. Talking about her in front of an audience of hundreds of thousands of people would be a nightmare for her. After all, she'd basically begged me not to talk to *any* reporters at the hospital. The resolute look in her eyes had told me how serious she was about the request. And now I was going to broadcast our situation around the state? But what the hell was I supposed to do? I had to find her. I was afraid for her safety. I was afraid for Joy. Surely she would forgive me when she finally regained her sensibilities.

A fiftysomething man wearing square-rimmed glasses stepped out of the studio and approached me in the hallway.

"Luke?"

"Yes."

"Doug Pederson. Good to meet you in person."

We shook quick hands. Doug was the producer I'd spoken with on the phone the night before.

"I guess you being here means nothing has changed?"

"Correct," I replied. "I still haven't heard from her."

"I'm sorry."

But I could almost see a slight sparkle in his eye, as if he were glad nothing had changed on my end because this was going to be a major segment on his TV show. I couldn't blame him. If this weren't happening to me, I'd also find the story enthralling: a hero who had rescued kids from a burning building and disappeared without a trace less than twenty-four hours later. Both Ashley and I would have stopped what we were doing in the bathroom to pay close attention to that story.

"We have about thirty minutes," Doug said. "We need to get you in front of our makeup gal. Don't worry, nothing too bad. Just a little powder here and there to make sure you look good on camera."

"Okay, sure."

I followed him down the hallway and into a room where several chairs were positioned in front of lit mirrors with all kinds of makeup and accessories. A fortysomething man in a solid-brown romper sat in one of the chairs. The patch on the front of the romper said DENVER ZOO. A girl with spiky pink-and-purple hair was poking at the guy's brown hair and putting everything in place.

"I need Mr. Driskell fixed up, Sheila," Doug said to her.

"No problem. Finishing up right now."

"I'll come back and get you in a few minutes," Doug said to me.

I nodded, stood there, watching another man get his hair and makeup done in front of me. This was an out-of-body experience. The guy in the chair glanced over at me.

"Not my favorite part," he said. "I'm more used to having elephant poop smeared on my face. But I guess this is part of the gig."

"I presume you work for the zoo?" I asked.

"Yep. They have me on once a month."

"Cool."

"What about you? Why're you on the show today?"

I wasn't sure what to say. How do you casually tell a stranger that you're living an absolute nightmare when you're about to sit in a chair and have your face powdered up?

"I'm here to talk about my wife. She rescued some kids from a fire two days ago."

"Over in Vail?" the makeup artist asked excitedly.

I nodded.

"I saw that on Twitter!" she exclaimed. "It was amazing. You must be so proud of your wife. Is she also here?"

"No, she's, uh . . . not."

I didn't feel like getting into it yet. I wanted to tell this story only once. And that was when the TV cameras were rolling.

Twenty minutes later, I was standing off to the side with some woman wearing a headset whose name I'd already forgotten. The two hosts were finishing up the segment with the zookeeper, who had brought out some weird lizards and snakes. They were smiling and making jokes, and I couldn't believe I was about to follow this up with something so damn serious. I felt out of place and kept glancing down at my phone, hoping a text would come in from Susan. I wanted to pull the plug on this right now. Susan had gone over to my house this morning after I'd left simply to wait there in case Ashley showed up. But I'd heard nothing from her.

It looked like this was happening. The segment with the zookeeper was over, and the smiles immediately vanished from the two hosts' faces when the show went to commercial. The girl in the headset ushered me up onto the stage and over to two nice chairs with a small table between them. She then made sure the mic they'd put on me was in place and working okay. I looked over and saw Doug Pederson speaking with the blonde host. I thought her name was Jessie something, but I couldn't remember. She glanced in my direction as Doug kept talking, gave me a sympathetic grin. I couldn't even grin back. It just felt inappropriate. Then the host walked over to the two chairs and found her place in the one opposite me.

"Hi, Luke. Jessie Markson."

"Nice to meet you."

But it wasn't nice. It was horrible. At least in this situation. I could see a digital clock on the wall, counting down. It was already at thirty seconds. In half a minute, I would open my whole life to anyone watching. I thought about Ashley and Joy, and reminded myself I was doing this for them. I was doing this for their own health and safety. I was doing this because I loved them so much. I was doing this to bring us all back together as a family.

Three . . . two . . . one.

Jessie, the host, began speaking to the camera. "Yesterday, we showed you the viral video of an incredibly brave woman in Vail who ran into a burning school building and single-handedly rescued eight schoolchildren."

I could see in monitors behind the cameras that the TV screen was split, showing Jessie on one side and the video of Ashley on the other.

Jessie continued, "Today, that story has taken a dramatic turn. Ashley Driskell, the woman in the video, has disappeared. We're joined today by her husband, Luke, who is in desperate need of your help."

She turned to me. My heart was beating so fast.

"Good morning, Luke. Thank you for being here."

"Thank you for having me."

"Tell us what happened."

"Well, Ashley was in the hospital recovering. And then she left in the middle of the night. I searched all day for her yesterday but never found her. She hasn't called or texted. And nobody in Vail has seen or heard from her. At least, none of the people I spoke with yesterday."

"And you also don't know the whereabouts of your stepdaughter?"

"Correct. When I got up yesterday morning, Joy was also gone."

I saw a photo I'd emailed Doug earlier of Ashley and Joy appear on the TV screen. Joy was eating a strawberry ice-cream cone. Ashley had her arms wrapped around Joy from behind and was leaning over to pose. Both had the biggest smiles on their faces. It damn near brought tears to my eyes. A caption below the photo said: Hero Missing.

"Are the police involved?" Jessie asked me.

"Yes, I spoke with the police yesterday."

"But they don't have any answers?"

"Not yet."

"Do you suspect foul play?"

"I have no reason to suspect that. But I don't know what to think. I'm at a loss about what has happened to them. That's why I'm here, seeking help."

"And we want to help," Jessie said, before turning to look at the camera again. "There's a number for the station on your screen right now. If you have any information about this situation, please call it. Help us find Ashley and Joy and bring them home." She looked back to me. "Is there anything else you'd like to say to our viewers?"

"Yes. I'm, uh, offering a reward for any leads that help us locate them."

"What kind of reward?"

"One million dollars."

I hadn't planned it. It just came to me in the moment, birthed out of the deepest and most desperate part of my soul. This was my best chance to find Ashley and Joy. I couldn't waste it. I had to somehow compel the audience into action. So I had to ask myself: How much would I be willing to pay right now if someone walked me down a path that led me straight to Ashley and Joy? Truth was, I would trade everything I had. But I knew that exact number would initiate the ripple I wanted. I could already tell by looking at Jessie, whose mouth had dropped open in shock. For a second, she was speechless. Behind the glaring lights, I could make out the same expressions on most of the others in the room.

Jessie quickly regained her composure. "There you go, ladies and gentlemen. Now you have a million reasons to call the number listed on your screen. We'll be right back."

The show went to commercial again.

Jessie turned to me again. "Are you serious?"

"Yes, I am."

"Wow. I'm just . . . stunned. I really hope it works, Luke."

"Me, too."

TWELVE

Back in Vail, I stood in my kitchen, watching the news unfold on the TV. Mark was on a stool at the island. He'd already made himself a screwdriver with orange juice from the fridge and expensive vodka from my liquor cabinet. I declined a drink, even though I probably could have used one. I was jittery. The morning's events at the TV station had shot a new course of adrenaline straight through me. But I needed to stay clearheaded. I had no idea what today would bring. I wanted to make sure I was ready for anything. Susan was standing in the living room, staring at the huge TV above the fireplace, flipping through the news channels. CNN. Fox News. MSNBC. Local news. In the past thirty minutes, each of them had mentioned my turn on the Denver TV show that morning.

The $1 million reward had driven the story forward in a way I could have never anticipated. I still felt stunned by what I'd done. A million dollars was a lot of money. I didn't know if it would work or just throw a wrench into my search. My phone was now constantly vibrating because so many texts and calls were coming in all at once. It seemed everyone I knew in Vail and the surrounding area was messaging me about Ashley, their concern, and—of course—their commitment to being on the lookout for her.

Doug Pederson, from the morning show, had told me the phone number they'd listed was already blowing up. It was a phone number set up with a voice mail asking people to leave a message with any information about Ashley and Joy. He had two interns monitoring the messages. I'd promised Doug an exclusive with whatever became of the story if they did the legwork on the calls. Doug said he'd reach out if anything worthwhile came from it. He expected most of the calls to be from kooks, especially with the big reward out there. But you never knew. It was worth a shot.

I called my assistant at my office in Palo Alto and asked her to cancel all my meetings the next few days. There was no way I was going to be able to work again until all this was resolved. It was a tough time to be away. I was currently overseeing development of several exciting new software projects focused on inner-city education in the poorest cities in the country. It was meaningful work. She said everyone was shocked and thinking about me. I then called my right-hand man on the projects. I told him to inform my team and encouraged him to stay focused on the task at hand. Finally, I sent a text to my two partners, updating them on my situation. Both told me to take whatever time I needed.

"You sure you don't want a drink?" Mark asked. "Calm the nerves?"

"I'm sure." I ran both hands through my hair, tugged on it in the back. "Did I do the right thing?"

"I think you did what any husband who loves his family would do if they had the same resources as you."

"She's going to hate me for it. Even if this works, she may never forgive me. She didn't even want me talking to reporters when it was just about what happened with her at the day-care facility."

"You can't worry about that right now. She'll forgive you. We just need to find her first and then deal with that on the other side."

"Right." I looked back up at the TV. There was yet another mention of my story on the screen. "I need some fresh air. I'm going to go for a walk."

"You want company?"

"No, bud, but thanks."

I stepped outside the front door of my house and noticed my neighbors from two doors down walking up the driveway. Chris and Sunni, a fiftysomething couple with two grown kids. I really didn't want to talk to them. I'd already had several people on my street stop by the house that morning, just trying to be nice and caring. Mark had handled most of it at the door for me. I considered turning around and going back inside, but it was too late. We'd already made eye contact. I could see their sad head tilts. It reminded me of how everyone had treated me for months after Jill was killed.

Jill and I were supposed to have attended a dinner function together that tragic night. It had been a fundraiser for San Francisco Ballet. Jill had helped organize it and had been looking forward to it for weeks. So she'd been extremely upset with me for skipping out last minute because I was trying to close on the potential acquisition of a smaller software company. They'd had a great product that we believed could be a major boost for us. I'd known she was going to be pissed, but I made the decision to stay in the meeting anyway.

The call had come in around ten thirty that night. I had pressed Decline on the same number several times, but they just kept incessantly ringing me. So I'd finally stepped out to answer it. It was the police. Jill had been shot and killed in a carjacking downtown. She'd been six months pregnant. One of the bullets had gone straight through her stomach. The baby was also dead. I'd felt a wave of anguish level me and put me on the floor for several minutes. Even thinking about it now was difficult. Jill should have never been in that position; I should have been behind the wheel of the car. If I had chosen her over business, it would have never happened. But I chose wrong. And my family had suffered unimaginable consequences.

"Hey, guys," I said, meeting my neighbors halfway up the driveway.

Chris spoke first. "We just wanted to stop by and say we're praying for you."

"Thank you. I appreciate it."

"What an awful situation," Sunni added.

"It is."

My answers were short and sweet; I was hoping they would take the hint. It wasn't that I didn't appreciate my neighbors' support—I did. I was just exhausted and didn't want to keep having these same conversations. We chatted a couple more minutes before they finally left. I followed a mountain trail off our street and began walking up the switchbacks. I took my phone with me, even though I was so tired of getting all the messages. I couldn't *not* have it on me. I hoped that Ashley would somehow see the news and call me. I'd even take her angrily screaming at me right now over not hearing from her at all. I kept repeatedly checking for her phone's GPS signal, but to no avail. Her Mazda was back in my garage; Mark had helped me get it last night. If she had access to a vehicle, she'd either borrowed one, stolen one, or somehow paid for it with the cash.

My phone buzzed again. The ID said VAIL POLICE DEPARTMENT.

I answered. "Hello?"

"Luke, this is Detective Livingston. We spoke yesterday."

"Yes."

"I just want you to know we're officially investigating your wife and stepdaughter's disappearance now."

"That's good to hear."

"Not sure you gave us much choice. We've been bombarded with calls ever since you went on TV this morning."

"Just doing whatever I can to find her."

"I understand. Can you come by the station? We'd like to go over everything with you again, just to get better bearings on the situation."

"Of course. I'll head right over."

I hung up, stared back down the mountain for a moment. I'd made it a good way up the trail and had a great view over the town. I took a deep breath and let it out slowly. My eyes shifted over so many familiar landmarks. *Where are you, Ashley? Why're you doing this? Why did you run? Did I do something to push you away? Are you okay? Is Joy? What has happened to you?* My breathing grew rapid. Everything I'd been holding so tightly inside me was suddenly flooding out. My chest seized up. I had no choice but to lie down right there in the grass by the hiking trail. I pulled my blue hoodie all the way up over my head to cover my face, trying to create a dark space that would block out the sky. I squeezed my eyes shut as hard as possible, focused on my breathing, trying to calm myself down. Eyes closed, I saw Ashley's face. She was looking at me and smiling. Her perfect smile. Nothing made me happier. She was wearing her favorite red sweater with the thick, high collar. I loved that sweater. Probably because it was the same one she'd been wearing when I proposed to her back in April.

A bad day that had turned out good.

We held hands and walked along the trail beside Gore Creek. The sun was out, but it was still a chilly April afternoon. The creek was flowing nicely and crackling in all the right spots. Ski season was over, but there were still patches of snow lingering around the banks of the water. While I enjoyed skiing and the majesty of a white winter, I loved summer in the mountains even more. The hiking, biking, fishing, and golfing . . . Nothing compared. I was really looking forward to making the turn this year. But it was more than just the warmer weather and fun activities; it was because of the woman walking next to me. We'd been dating seven months, and I was all in with Ashley. Was she all in with me? It felt like it.

"Joy wants to start taking ballet lessons," she said.

"Really? She would look so cute in a tutu skirt."

"She watched the movie Barbie in the Nutcracker *the other day, and it's all she's been talking about. She keeps spinning and leaping around our apartment. And bumping into our furniture and walls."*

I laughed. "Your place is not exactly fit for a dance studio."

She smiled. "No, it's not. But that's not stopping her."

"When that little girl wants something, she just goes for it."

"Yes, she does."

I turned to her. "What about her mom?"

She looked up at me. "What?"

"When her mom wants something, does she go for it?"

Ashley sighed. "Less and less. When you have a child, you have to measure your risks."

"True. But that doesn't mean you take no risks."

"Standing here, holding your hand, is a big risk for me."

I pitched my head. "Why?"

I could tell she wanted to say something, but she didn't. It always felt that way with her. Every time she seemed to be on the verge of sharing something important with me, she held it back.

"It's complicated," she said.

"Does it have to be?"

"Yes," she answered definitively. "Life makes it that way."

"You know I'm in love with you, right?"

She gave me a small smile. "I know."

"Do you feel the same?"

She took a deep breath and let it out slowly. I could feel my heart pumping. It was the first time I'd put it out there so openly. I'd whispered that I loved her a couple of times in the past month, but I still had not heard it back from her. When she didn't respond right away, I jumped back in.

"Let me guess: it's complicated."

I saw tears in her eyes. "I'm afraid to love anyone."

"Because of your childhood?"

We had talked about how hard it was growing up in foster care. Never knowing your parents. Always feeling abandoned. Never feeling like she could trust anyone. Which was why I never pressed her too hard to share before she was ready. I could never imagine the pain of bouncing through multiple foster homes and, at times, being abused both emotionally and physically in horrific ways. She deserved my patience, even if I had to offer it over a lifetime together.

"Yes. And . . ." She again paused.

"What is it, Ashley? What're you not telling me?"

"If you knew everything about me, you'd probably leave."

"No, I wouldn't."

"Don't say that, Luke. You don't know."

"You're wrong. I know it in the deepest parts of my heart and soul. Nothing you could say would change my mind. And I'll prove it to you."

"How?"

I reached my hand into my coat pocket and found the small jewelry box I'd been carrying around with me for a few weeks, looking for the right moment. I didn't know it would be today. I didn't know it would be right now. But I could feel every part of me saying now. *This was the woman. This was the moment. It was time to put it all out there. I knelt on one knee in front of her, pulled out the jewelry box, and opened it. Inside was my mother's engagement ring. It was nothing fancy—a tiny diamond set in an ornate antique band. I knew better by now than to buy Ashley a huge diamond ring and try to wow her with the number of carats. I saw Ashley's eyes go wide; a small gasp came from her lips. I couldn't tell if it was a good or bad sign.*

"I'll never leave you, Ashley. I knew you were the one after the first day I met you at the art festival last year. I've known with each moment we've shared together over the past few months. I don't think I've felt more certain about anything in my life up to this point. I love you. And I love Joy like my own child. You're my everything. And I want to commit the rest of my life to making you feel as safe and loved as possible. Will you marry me?"

Ashley's tears were flowing now. But I also saw fear in her eyes.

"I don't . . . I don't know what to say, Luke."

I felt a knot in my throat. "You don't love me?"

"Of course I love you! If you knew how much, it might scare you."

That felt good to hear. "Then say yes."

"I . . . I can't. I'm sorry."

"I don't understand." I slowly stood, feeling so damn confused and frustrated over the mixed response from her. "What is it?"

She looked paralyzed. I'd never seen this look on her face before. I don't think I fully understood the depth of her abandonment pain.

"I have to go. I'm so sorry, Luke."

And with that, I watched her quickly walk away from me down the path. And she never looked back. I was certain in that moment it was over between us. The look in her eyes told me she would never get over whatever was holding her back from me. I was absolutely crushed and had no idea how I would get past it. But I didn't have to remain in that place for too long. Ashley showed up on my doorstep later that night.

"Hey," I said, shocked to see her.

I could tell she had been crying, because her eyes were completely bloodshot. So were mine. She got right to it.

"Would you leave behind everything for me?" she asked. "All of this, Luke. The house, the lifestyle, all of it."

"Why are you—"

"Please just tell me the truth."

"Of course I would."

"Are you sure? Be certain. Would you move across the world for me?"

"Ashley, what—"

"Just tell me."

"Yes, the answer is one hundred percent yes."

"What if we had to live in a shack in the woods?"

I had so many questions, but now was clearly not the time. "I'd go anywhere to be with you and Joy. I promise. I'd choose us. Always."

She let out a slow breath; a small smile touched her lips. "Then my answer is yes. I will marry you."

My heart nearly exploded in my chest. I swept her up in my arms, spinning her around in a circle as I hugged her tightly, my lips fully embraced with hers. I could feel a palpable tension in her body releasing as I held her so close to me. I finally set her down.

"Let's do it right away," she said.

"Really? What about planning, dresses, flowers—"

"I don't want any of that. I just want you, me, and Joy. Maybe a couple of friends. I'll ask our pastor to do a private ceremony in the church garden."

"Okay. Sounds perfect."

THIRTEEN

My hope that my reward-money offer would somehow lead to a more immediate resolution faded with each passing hour. I spent two hours with the police, going over every detail of what had happened the past two days, and even connected them with Doug Pederson, who had a growing list of mostly nonsensical voice mails from people who claimed they'd either spotted Ashley or knew critical information. Some calls came from faraway places like Canada and even Ireland. The detective seemed annoyed at having to deal with the TV station. He said if Ashley and Joy were already in a foreign country, there was nothing they could do about it. Nor was there any motivation on their part if she'd chosen to go there on her own. The detective reminded me that they were not a domestic-counseling service. There were no signs of foul play. No indications that Ashley and Joy had been kidnapped or taken against their will. Everything to this point led them to believe Ashley had intentionally left. That was not a crime, no matter how heartbroken I felt about the whole thing. Joy was technically her daughter and not mine. While the detective said they would be investigating, I didn't walk out of the police station feeling great about the lengths they would go to find my family.

Because I couldn't stand the thought of sitting around my home all day waiting for something to happen, I began making my own sweep through town again—a pointless exercise, considering everyone was now on the lookout for Ashley. But this became even more difficult when everyone recognized me from TV—something that Susan said had also gone viral on social media. I was a pariah walking down the paver streets of Vail Village as everyone stopped and stared at me. *There goes that sad million-dollar man.* I felt like a prisoner in my own community. I didn't want to be at home, but I also didn't want to be out among the people.

I kept replaying in my mind every detail of the few days before Ashley had vanished to see if I could remember any signs or clues that something was not right with us. Had she been acting different? Had I said or done anything that could have possibly caused this? But there was nothing. We'd been completely in sync. The night before the fire rescue, we'd had a nice romantic dinner at home. I had made chicken parmesan, pasta, and salad, one of her favorite meals, and we enjoyed it with wine over candlelight while Joy was asleep in her bedroom. This eventually led to us moving to our own bedroom. If there was any possible disconnect between us, Ashley sure didn't act like it. We were a husband and wife enjoying every part of each other. Mind, body, and soul. There was no possible way for me to wrap my mind around her leaving me a little more than twenty-four hours later. I also kept thinking about my time with her in the hospital after I'd mentioned the TV reporters. I'd noticed that fear-driven look in her eyes. She'd immediately wanted me to go get Joy. Why?

My phone buzzed, just like it'd been doing every few minutes all day. I wished I could turn it off, because it was driving me crazy hearing from so many people unrelated to finding Ashley and Joy. But I couldn't. Not when I was desperately clinging to hope that I would eventually see her name on the screen. That she'd finally snapped back to reality.

But every time I looked at my phone, these hopes were crushed. It was like being constantly jabbed with a needle all day long. I was worn out.

This call was from Vail Health Hospital. I decided to answer.

"This is Luke."

"Hey, Luke, this is Dr. Longview. Sorry to bother you. I'm sure this has been a long day for you already."

"No, it's okay. What is it?"

"I'm not sure, to be honest. After you went on TV this morning, I just felt this gut instinct to look deeper into Ashley's time here with us. So I went back to the security videos and searched through the hours right before she walked out of her hospital room. I found something disturbing."

I perked up. "What?"

"Well, a man in scrubs came into her room about thirty minutes before she left. He was only in there a few minutes. Because we don't have cameras in the rooms, I have no idea what happened in there."

"Who was he?"

"That's the thing—he's not anyone on our staff. I've asked around, and no one recognizes him. As a matter of fact, nobody even remembers seeing him in the building that night."

"What did he look like?"

"Asian. Short black hair, trim build. Clean cut. Probably in his thirties, I would guess."

I immediately thought of the FBI agent—Special Agent Chang—whom I'd spoken with outside the hospital yesterday morning.

"Can I come see the security video for myself?"

"Of course."

I stood in the same security room as I had yesterday, with the same guard working the monitors. Dr. Longview was standing next to me. They'd had everything cued up and ready for me upon my arrival. The guard pressed a few buttons on his keyboard and the video played, showing the hallway right outside Ashley's hospital room. A guy suddenly appeared. As Dr. Longview had mentioned, he was wearing blue scrubs, with a stethoscope around his neck, and holding a clipboard in his hand. He looked hospital official. But it was definitely Agent Chang. My heart started racing. I watched as he casually but carefully moved through the hallway and then stepped inside Ashley's room. Precisely four minutes later, he poked his head out of the room, made sure no one was in clear view, and then quickly walked away.

"I recognize him," I said.

"You do?" asked the doctor.

"Yeah. He's an FBI agent. He stopped me outside the hospital yesterday morning, said he was investigating the school fire for possible arson. Can you show me how he entered and exited the building?"

The guard quickly cued it up. The FBI agent entered through the main glass doors. He did it when the receptionist was not behind the main desk. He was already in the blue scrubs. Agent Chang moved, in quick but measured fashion, past the big lobby desk and down the hallway. He raised a security card at a secured door and then pushed through. It seemed clear to me he was looking to avoid contact with anyone at the hospital, but not to the point where he was hiding around corners. Moving toward the corridor where Ashley was in her room, the agent slowed in certain places and then moved quickly in others—always avoiding the hospital staff. It was not too difficult. The corridor was not busy. Agent Chang did the same thing on the way out. He hovered a moment in the lobby, his eyes on his clipboard for a few minutes, until the receptionist was distracted by something in a file cabinet behind her. Then he breezed past her and exited the building.

The guard spoke up. "The security card he used belonged to Nurse Margaret. She came in yesterday and told me she'd somehow misplaced her card, so I issued her a new one and canceled her old one."

"That's odd," Dr. Longview said. "I wonder how he got it from her. And why would an FBI agent sneak into our building like that?"

I had no idea, but my mind was spinning sideways. Agent Chang had lied to me. He'd told me he hadn't spoken with Ashley yet. But he clearly had. In secret. Why? And why had Ashley bolted from the building thirty minutes after he left her room? It didn't make any sense. Was Chang really a federal agent? I couldn't be sure without speaking to someone from the FBI. Which was what I planned to do next.

FOURTEEN

A quick online search showed a local satellite FBI office over in Avon, ten miles up the road from Vail. Instead of calling the office number, I decided to drive straight there, in hopes of speaking to someone in person. If Agent Chang was legitimate, I didn't want to alert him in advance of my visit. I just wanted to show up so he wouldn't have time to come up with a cover for his story. He'd lied to me once; I had no doubt he would continue to lie to me. Not that the FBI had to tell me anything. But I knew I had a better chance at getting the truth in an abrupt face-to-face conversation. I was convinced whatever had happened between him and Ashley that night in the hospital had clearly pushed her to run. Not only to run that night but to stay in hiding, without any communication with me, even as a statewide search was going on because of the money I had put up to find her.

Ashley was afraid. Why?

The FBI office was at the end of a nondescript one-story gray-brick building that also housed a dry cleaner, liquor store, and yoga studio. It was not marked as an FBI office—no Federal Bureau of Investigation seal on the door or anything like that. Just a unit number. No one would know it was an FBI office if they hadn't looked up the address. That probably kept the wackos from showing up all the time.

I parked in the small lot outside the building strip and approached the black-tinted front glass door. I couldn't see inside. My nerves felt jittery. Something told me this was about to take a dramatic turn. I just didn't know in what direction.

I reached down, tried to tug the front door open. I cursed; it was locked. I knocked on the door several times. No one came to answer. I cupped both hands against the glass and tried to see inside. I could make out that the lights were on, and I thought I saw someone moving around. So I knocked again, this time dragging it out in an obnoxious fashion. When I thought I'd made it clear I was not leaving, someone finally came to the door. I heard the lock unlatch, and then a guy in a white polo and black slacks pulled the door open. He was probably a few years younger than me, late twenties, with short-cropped brown hair and a neatly trimmed beard.

"Can I help you?" he asked, looking irritated.

"Is this the FBI office?"

His eyes narrowed. "Who's asking?"

"My name is Luke Driskell, and I'm—"

"Wait, you're the guy who was on TV this morning, right? The million-dollar guy with the missing wife?"

It felt strange to hear someone sum up my life that way.

"Yes, I am."

"That's a bizarre deal. I'm Special Agent Danny Lamar. What can I do for you?"

"I need your help."

"Your situation is not really FBI related. More of a police matter."

"Then why did an FBI agent question me yesterday?"

He cocked his head. "What FBI agent?"

"Special Agent Chang."

His face wrinkled up. "Who? I don't know any Special Agent Chang. It's only me and Special Agent Shaw who operate out of this small satellite office. And Shaw is currently gone on a fishing trip."

"He showed me an official FBI badge. At least, I thought it was official."

"All right, come inside. Let's talk this through."

Agent Lamar opened the door, allowed me in, and then shut and locked it behind me. There wasn't much to the office space, although it was clean and tidy. A desk sat in each corner of the room with guest chairs in front of it. Two huge whiteboards on opposite walls with scribblings all over them. A hallway toward the back. I could see what looked like a small kitchen.

"You want some coffee or something?" the FBI agent asked.

"No, I'm good."

"Smart call. Shaw buys the worst coffee on the planet. I can barely get it down." He motioned toward a chair in front of one of the desks. "Have a seat, Luke. You mind if I call you that?"

"Sure."

"You can call me Danny. You look familiar to me. And it's not just from spotting you on TV this morning. Have we met before?"

"I don't believe so."

He studied me a longer moment. "I swear we have. Where are you from?"

"Just outside San Antonio."

"I grew up in Dallas."

"I didn't spend much time in Dallas."

"Yeah, it wasn't there." He twisted his mouth up, still thinking. Then it apparently dawned on him. "Wait, did you play basketball in college?"

This surprised me. "Yeah, I did. At Rice University, a decade ago."

He snapped his fingers, pointed at me. "Bingo, that's it! Conference USA tournament. I played guard at SMU. We faced each other in the semifinals. I remember you went eight for eight from the free throw line in the final two minutes to clinch the win and beat us by a point. I hated you that day."

Now it all came back to me, too. "Danny Lamar. I remember. You fouled me so hard on a layup that I ended up in the bleachers and thought I had a concussion."

He laughed. "Sorry about that."

"Wow. Now you're an FBI agent."

He shrugged. "Well, the NBA wasn't really interested in a slow-footed five-nine guy with a below-average jumper."

"Yeah, I hear ya. Same with me."

"Man, what a small world. I'd ask how you're doing, Luke, but it's clear your life is a bit of a car wreck right now."

"You could say that again."

"Well, sit down, and let me try to help."

He had an easygoing way about him that I immediately liked. I sat in the guest chair while he went around and took his chair on the other side. Two large computer monitors were on the desktop.

"All right, tell me more about this Chang guy."

"Asian. My guess is young thirties. Clean-cut, short black hair. He was wearing a black sport coat. He walked up to me when I was leaving the hospital yesterday morning."

I pulled up a photo I'd snapped of Chang from the hospital security video on my phone and showed it to Danny.

"Don't recognize him," Danny said. "You get a first name?"

"No, I didn't. I honestly barely looked at his badge."

Danny began typing on his keyboard, eyes on his screen. He studied his monitor for a few moments. "We have several Changs with the Bureau. Tommy Chang out of New York City. Han Chang in San Francisco. Jiro Chang in Boston." He turned one of his monitors to face me. "Any of these guys look like the guy you spoke with yesterday?"

I studied the faces. "No. He's not any of them."

He turned the screen back. "Wouldn't make much sense for one of these guys to come to town without us being alerted of it."

"He said he was with the Houston office for a little while. But he didn't indicate how long ago."

"Couldn't have been that long, if he's early thirties. I know someone in Houston. Let me give him a quick call."

Danny was on the phone with a guy a few seconds later, telling him the situation. He looked over at me, shook his head. He then thanked the guy and hung up.

"My guy has been in Houston for nearly a decade. He says they've never had an Agent Chang in their office while he's been there."

"So what does this mean?"

"I don't know. Why don't you tell me everything that happened?"

I put it all out there, starting with the fire rescue at the school, and then walked him through the horrific last thirty-six hours of my life that had led me to his front door today.

"Dang, Luke," Danny said. "This is crazy."

"Yeah, it is," I agreed. "So clearly this guy is not a real FBI agent."

"I can't completely verify that just yet. It's not like I'm high up on the food chain, or else I wouldn't be sitting in a remote office in a small town like this one. It's possible, if improbable, that some kind of clandestine operation is going on, and Agent Shaw and I are being kept in the dark."

I scoffed. "How could my wife possibly be involved with a clandestine FBI operation? Ashley is just a local painter."

Danny went back to his computer. "How do you spell her first name?"

I told him. He began typing and squinted at his screen. "Did she take your last name?"

"Yes. Why?"

"I don't see anyone listed in the area under that name. I do have several popping up in other parts of the country."

"She probably hasn't updated her driver's license yet."

"Did you turn in your marriage license?"

"Yes. Well, *she* did."

He continued to type and search his screens. "It's not coming up."

"Maybe she forgot to turn it in. She can be a bit scatterbrained at times. Try her maiden name. Ashley Tolly."

"T-o-l-l-y?"

"Yes."

His eyes were darting back and forth down his screen. "How long has she lived in Colorado?"

"Four years."

"You said she was twenty-six?"

"Correct."

"What month was she born?"

"November twenty-ninth."

"Does she have an active driver's license?"

"Yes. Why? What's going on, Danny?"

Danny slowly eased back in his chair, considered his words a moment. "Look, man, I don't exactly know how to tell you this, so I'm just going to come straight out with it: the wife you know doesn't exist."

FIFTEEN

I felt gut punched. How could this even be possible? How could the woman I'd married not actually exist? Ashley had a Colorado driver's license. I'd seen it plenty of times with my own eyes. She still got carded here and there when ordering wine or cocktails. I'd even told her the photo on the license was the most attractive I'd ever seen. But Danny was insistent that the driver's license wasn't legit. The Colorado DMV had no account for it. And there was nothing in the FBI's official database.

Ashley Tolly of Eagle, Colorado, was not a real person.

And neither was Special Agent Chang.

I had to believe those two things were somehow connected. But how would Ashley have even gotten a fake driver's license? You can't just order one off Amazon—at least, not if you want it to look and feel real. I'd held Ashley's driver's license in my own hands. It looked and felt real in every possible way. I knew anything was possible with technology these days—college kids could pull off this kind of thing—but my wife hardly ever used a computer.

I remembered I had done a Google search on Ashley after meeting her last year. I'd found nothing on her other than a few online hits from the past two years. Most of those had been listings from various art shows and events. But there had been nothing before that. I hadn't thought too much of it at the time. Especially after I'd found out she'd never used any social media.

I drove home feeling like my world was suddenly spinning out of control. But I was also even more determined to find the truth. Ashley was in trouble. She hadn't run because she had a concussion or a paranoid reaction from her pain medication. She hadn't run because she was leaving me. Ashley had run because she was afraid of something. She'd run because she was in danger. Everything inside me told me that was the truth.

It was the only truth that made any sense. But it scared the hell out of me. What could Ashley be so afraid of that she wouldn't allow me to protect her and Joy? I had access to the best lawyers. I had the money to hire an army of security guys. Why had she cut me out of it? I suddenly felt uneasy about what I'd done that morning at the TV station. By dropping a spotlight on Ashley, could I have possibly put her in even more danger?

I got home, pulled into the garage, and walked into my empty house. I had moved beyond any hope of finding Ashley and Joy suddenly back home. That optimism had already died. I walked straight to my liquor cabinet and poured myself a small glass of bourbon. I took it down in one full gulp. I needed help in taking the edge off. I couldn't waste time dealing with more anxiety attacks. I then began listening to the dozens of voice mails that had come in on my phone since I'd been at the FBI office. Danny said he'd continue to investigate the matter. After all, impersonating an FBI agent was a federal crime. So that gave him a reason to be involved.

Most of the messages were from friends and acquaintances. The police detective gave me a quick update that basically said they still had nothing. And Doug Pederson at the TV station revealed the same thing. Ashley was nowhere to be found. Where could she and Joy have gone? Where could they be hiding? And how could they have gone for this long without anyone seeing them or talking to them? Ashley wasn't some kind of secret agent. She wasn't trained to operate as a ghost. But then, what was the truth and what wasn't? She'd lied to me about her real name. She could have lied to me about everything else. I wanted to pour myself another glass of bourbon but resisted the urge. This was no time to get drunk.

I took a deep breath and let it out slowly. I tried to calm myself down and began running everything that had happened back through my mind. What all did I know so far? Ashley had acted weird about the mention of reporters while I was with her in the hospital. She'd immediately wanted me to go get Joy. Had that been because she was afraid for Joy's safety? My wife had bolted out of the hospital right after the fake FBI agent visited her. What had he said that made her do something like that? Had he threatened her? Who was he? I began to go back through every detail of my exchange with him.

Then I sat for a minute on one of the final questions he'd asked.

"The little girl, Joy. She is your stepdaughter?"

"Yes."

"Where is her real father?"

"He died before she was born."

Why had the guy asked about Joy's real father? Could all this be connected to her dead father? Was Chang someone from that family? Could Ashley have run from that situation for some reason she'd never told me about? I admittedly knew very few details about what had happened. Ashley had said she'd met a guy while living in Laguna Beach. She'd moved out there from Virginia when she was twenty-two because she had a friend who offered to put her up in a guest room, and Laguna Beach was known for its art scene. The guy had owned an art studio. She'd allowed herself to get swept up while in a vulnerable state, and it had resulted in an unexpected pregnancy. She'd had no intention to marry the guy—she wasn't going to let one mistake compound into two. She hadn't even wanted to tell the guy, even though she knew she had to do it. But she'd never gotten the chance. The guy had died in a car accident. Then Ashley had moved.

Was that the truth? Or was there more to it?

I moved down the hallway and into my home office, where I sat at my desk and opened my laptop. What was the guy's name? I knew his last name was Lin; I remembered that much. But I couldn't recall his first name. I opened Google on my screen, typed *Lin*, *Laguna Beach*, and *obituary*. This didn't get me too far. I added the year Ashley had said she was there. Four years ago. Then I scrolled and found something. An article from the *Orange County Register* titled "Man Left Bar, Was Never Seen Alive Again." This made me perk up. The article said a man named Kai Lin had left a Laguna Beach bar and vanished into the darkness on a cold January night. I now remembered Ashley telling me this specific name. This was the guy. The article went on to say he was missing for three days while his family and friends searched for him. Then his body had been found floating in Crescent Bay. The coroner had concluded that he'd been shot through the back multiple times. Police were still searching for answers. The article said Kai Lin was thirty-eight and a well-liked local art-gallery owner. There was a photo of him standing in front of his gallery. I continued to search, wondering if the police had ever solved the murder. But I couldn't find anything online that said anyone was ever arrested. It looked like it was still an open case.

I pushed back from my desk, trying to take this all in. This had to be Joy's father. Everything lined up except for one thing: Ashley had said he'd died in a car accident, not that he'd been murdered. My mind immediately started running with crazy scenarios. Could Ashley have somehow been involved in the murder of Joy's father? Even thinking that felt completely ridiculous. There was no way. But still, why would she lie about his death? Was it to protect Joy? Or was it something else? What did all this mean? And where did I go from here?

I took a deep breath and quickly settled it in my mind.

I had to go to Laguna Beach.

SIXTEEN

I called my representative at the private airline company my partners and I used for travel to find out how quickly he could get me on a plane to Laguna Beach. He told me they currently had a plane at Denver International, and he just needed to confirm if a pilot was available. I told him money was no object; I would gladly pay an expedited fee. My rep called me back ten minutes later and said the pilot would pick me up in an hour. This was one of the perks of my newfound wealth: it made travel so much easier. I needed to start finding answers and couldn't stand the thought of sitting around the house anymore, waiting for a phone call that may never come. Something inside me told me Ashley had run because of what had happened in Laguna Beach four years ago. I needed to go find out.

While putting my laptop into my leather bag, I found a Barbie doll inside. It immediately brought tears to my eyes. I remembered I'd stuck it in my bag the other day, when Joy and I had left a playground. While I desperately missed my wife, I also badly missed my stepdaughter. She had also become my everything. Was she okay? Was she confused? Was she scared? I knew one thing for sure: Ashley would protect her fiercely. I'd learned that the hard way two months ago.

"What is wrong with you?" Ashley screamed at me the moment I walked into the house from the garage. She raced over to Joy, who had been with me, and pulled her in so tight I thought she might choke her.

"What do you mean?" I asked, confused. "What's going on?"

I could see now that her eyes were bloodshot. She'd been crying hard. And she was completely out of breath.

She gave me another stern look. One mixed with pulsing fear and deep anger. "I went to pick her up from the day camp an hour ago, but she wasn't there. They told me her father got her. But I've been freaking out because I thought you were in San Francisco."

"I came home early," I explained. "I left you a voice mail."

"I didn't get it. And I've been trying to call you!"

I pulled my phone out of my pocket, looked at the screen. My shoulders sagged. "I'm sorry. I placed my phone on Do Not Disturb during my meeting today and never switched it back."

"Mommy, it's okay," Joy said to Ashley. "We went to get ice cream."

Ashley squeezed her again, then told her go play with her dolls upstairs. Once we were alone, she turned back to me, still looking so pissed.

"You can never do that again, Luke," she said.

"Ashley, it was clearly unintentional. A set of unfortunate circumstances."

"Never again, okay? I need to know where she is at all times."

"I'm sorry it scared you."

But she wasn't interested in my apology, even if I thought it was unwarranted.

"Just say it won't happen again."

"Okay, it won't happen again. I'll make sure you know next time."

She wore a look I'd never seen on her face before. To me, it seemed way beyond that of an overprotective mother. This was something much different.

"I'm sorry," she finally said, after taking a breath and trying to calm herself down. "It's just . . . I'm not used to this. It's only been me and Joy for so long. Sharing her is all new to me. Plus, we've never done that day camp

before, so they don't know you. I was certain you weren't in town. So I was just scared that some stranger had abducted Joy."

She came over to me and hugged me. I hugged her back, kissed the top of her head. But I couldn't shake the feeling that look was more than her just being scared.

It was the look of terror.

That heated exchange took on a new meaning to me today. Maybe Ashley hadn't been afraid some stranger had abducted her daughter—maybe she'd been afraid someone she knew had taken Joy. Someone she'd been hiding from. Someone scary enough for her to change her entire identity and move a thousand miles away. I needed to find out. I drove to the Eagle airport and boarded the private plane after it arrived. Two hours later we were landing at John Wayne Airport in Orange County, about fifteen miles from Laguna Beach. It was nearing five o'clock. I grabbed an Uber and headed straight into the heart of Laguna Beach, where I was dropped a block from the ocean, in front of a bar called the Saloon. According to the article I'd found online, this was the last place Kai Lin had been seen on the night he disappeared.

I could see the beach up ahead of me on the left. There were people in swimsuits out, playing beach volleyball, riding bikes, and walking around. It was summer and the beach was happening. I went inside the bar and was surprised to find it already half-full. The Saloon was a small brick-walled pub with a dark-wood bar. It had a warm and easygoing atmosphere. I found my way over to a place at the bar. A guy who looked to be in his late thirties, with long shaggy hair and a beard, was whipping up cocktails and beers for everyone. He eventually made it over to me.

"What can I get you?"

"A glass of your favorite bourbon."

He laughed. "You know, if you leave that up to a bartender, he's going to go straight to the most expensive bottle."

"That's fine with me."

He smiled wide. "All right, dude. Coming right up!"

I looked around and wondered if Ashley used to come in here. What had life been like for her here in Laguna Beach, before she became a mother? Had she dated a lot? Did she used to have a wild side to her? Laguna clearly had a party vibe to it, although it was hard for me to imagine Ashley dancing in the clubs. That was just not her. At least, I didn't think it was her. But what did I really know about my wife? She'd changed her name. Had she changed everything else about herself?

The bartender came back with a glass. "Weller 12, my man. It's special."

I picked up the glass, took a sip, felt the kick. "I like it."

"I knew you would."

"How long you been bartending here?"

"About five years."

This was a plus. I needed to talk to someone who might have been around when Kai Lin had gone missing from here.

"You mind if I ask you a couple of questions about something that happened around here a few years ago?"

"After what you just ordered, ask away."

"Four years ago, a guy named Kai Lin disappeared after he left the Saloon. They found him shot dead in the ocean a few days later. You remember that?"

"Of course. It was the talk of the town for a while."

"Did you know him?"

"I mean, he was a regular. Probably came in twice a week or so. But I didn't *know* him know him."

"Were you working the night he disappeared?"

"Yep. Had to sit down with the cops to share with them everything that happened that night." His eyes narrowed. "Are you a reporter or something?"

"No, I'm just looking for someone. There's a chance it might be related." I picked my phone up off the bar, pulled up a photo of Ashley, and showed it to him. "Does this woman look familiar to you?"

He leaned in and took a good look. "Nah, sorry."

"She never came in here with the guy?"

"Nah, man. Believe me, I'd remember. She's hot."

"Okay, thanks." I took another sip. "They ever find out what happened?"

"To Kai Lin?" He shook his head. "Never. But there were rumors."

"What kind of rumors?"

"Several. Some thought he was involved with a Chinese criminal syndicate out of San Francisco. Or he was smuggling illegal immigrants into the country. There was even a rumor he was in conflict with another art-gallery owner about something. None of these have ever proven to be true."

"What do *you* think happened?"

He shrugged. "He was probably just randomly shot."

My gut said otherwise. I finished off my glass and felt the burn. Then I paid the bartender and headed to my next stop.

SEVENTEEN

The art gallery Kai Lin had started five years ago, according to a search on Google, was only a few blocks away, situated in a popular strip of other retail shops and art venues. The sign above the door said SAGE. It was fortunately still open when I got there. I walked inside through glass doors, finding white walls and displays covered with contemporary avant-garde paintings. Modern, pop, and street art. I only knew this because Ashley had been educating me on different art styles. I'd enjoyed getting more entrenched in her world. When she talked about art, her whole face lit up. And nothing pleased me more than seeing her come alive. Classical music played from speakers hidden somewhere above me. No one was currently in the gallery other than a man behind a white counter in the back corner. Wearing a sharp blue suit, he looked to be in his midthirties, with long black hair to his shoulders and stylish black spectacles. After spotting me, he came out from behind the counter and casually approached.

"Let me know if I can help you with anything," he said.

"I'm hoping you can. But it's not about art."

His forehead bunched. "Okay."

"I'm trying to find someone important to me. She used to live in Laguna Beach a few years ago."

I pulled out my phone, selected a photo of Ashley, and showed it to him.

"Amy," he said, his whole face smiling. "It's Amy."

"Why're you smiling?"

"Because she was so delightful. Her hair is dark here. But she was a blonde when I knew her."

I'd never seen Ashley as a blonde, not even in photos she had from before I knew her. She'd always had dark hair.

"Are you sure it's the same person?"

"Oh, absolutely. Amy was unforgettable. She worked with us part-time for a couple of months. Seeing this photo makes me sad."

"Why?"

"Because I never even got a chance to say goodbye to her, she moved away so fast. And I never heard from her again. I tried to find her a couple of times—you know, social media searches and whatnot—but I never could."

"Why were you trying to find her?"

"For one, she was a sweetheart, and I missed her. But she was also very close with the owner of the gallery."

"Kai Lin?"

He nodded. "Yes."

That connected with what I already knew. At least there was some truth to what Ashley had told me. I refused to think of her as anyone other than Ashley. I did not know Amy—nor did I want to know her. I'd married Ashley.

"Do you remember her last name?" I asked.

His eyes narrowed on me. "She's important to you, but you don't know her last name?"

I forced a quick, disarming smile, trying not to look overly suspicious. But this guy calling my wife Amy had brought on a surge of adrenaline. I wanted more answers. And I wanted them fast. But I needed to be patient with my approach.

"It's a little complicated," I admitted. "She changed her name."

"Really? Why? She had such a wonderful name—Amy Sundown. It fit her. Because she was as beautiful as a sunset. How is she?"

I wasn't sure what to tell him. So I stuck to the most basic facts. "She got married and has a three-year-old child."

I watched to see if my mentioning a child would register anything with this guy. Had he been close with Kai Lin? Did he know what had happened between Kai and Ashley and the pregnancy? But he didn't respond in any peculiar way that told me he knew about the baby.

"That's great. She deserves to be happy." He tilted his head. "But you said you were trying to find her?"

"Yes. I've lost communication with her."

"Are you a friend? Family?"

"Family."

I didn't feel like revealing more than that. I didn't want to further complicate the discussion.

"Do you think she came back to Laguna Beach?" he asked.

"Maybe. I can't say for sure. But that's why I'm here."

"I see. Well, I haven't seen her. But I would love to."

"You said she was close to the owner?"

He nodded. "Yes. Kai took her in like his own. She was in some kind of situation where he was trying to help her. I'm not sure what happened. Kai died before I ever got any of the details. And Amy left right after that."

"I read about what happened with Kai. Such a tragedy."

"Yes, it was. *Is.*" He sighed. "I'm still heartbroken."

"I read the police never arrested anyone. What do you think happened?"

"I've spent a lot of time trying to figure it out. But I still feel lost. He was the gentlest soul around. Never harmed or offended anyone."

"Did Kai have family around here?"

"No, not here. He had an uncle in New York City. But that's all. The rest of his family are all still in Beijing."

I thought about that. Agent Chang couldn't be Kai's uncle: the man was much younger looking than Kai himself. So why had Chang asked about him? I pulled up the photo I'd taken of Chang from the security video.

"Do you recognize this man?"

He squinted, then shook his head. "I do not."

I was getting nowhere fast. How was this all connected?

"Do you know how long Kai and Amy were seeing each other?"

He looked up at me and kind of laughed. "Excuse me?"

"They were an item at one point, right?"

"No, they were never seeing each other, my friend. At least, not in the sense of what I assume you're suggesting."

"Really? Could they have had a secret fling?"

He smiled wide. "No."

I was confused by his certainty. "How can you be so sure?"

"Because Kai was gay. And we'd been partners for five years."

EIGHTEEN

I flew home more baffled than ever. Why had Ashley told me Kai Lin was Joy's father? Why would she make up something like that? If he wasn't the father, then who was? Had Ashley been trying to keep me from ever finding out the truth? I couldn't be certain of her motivations. But I also couldn't get my mind off the fact that Chang had directly asked about Joy's father. This was clearly connected to that. I decided that when I got home, I would search through all Ashley's and Joy's belongings to see if could discover anything. To this point, I'd had no reason to question anything she'd told me about Joy's father. And certainly no motivation to dig deeper. Ashley must've had a good reason for making up her story about Kai Lin. She had to have been protecting Joy. She had to have been protecting me. But from whom and what?

I spent the majority of the two-hour flight home reading text messages and listening to countless voice mails left by friends and business associates—some people I hadn't heard from in years. I called Mark and Susan and got them caught up on my trip. Then I called Doug Pederson and got updated on the tip-line response. He told me plenty of calls claiming the callers had spotted Ashley all over the country continued to come in. But still, nothing seemed legitimate. Most of the photos sent in by eyewitnesses looked nothing at all like Ashley. Finally, I called the detective from Vail Police, who pretty much gave me the same report. Nothing positive had come from my time on TV that morning. It was shocking to me. Were Ashley and Joy really that good at hiding? Or had someone already taken them?

After landing at the Eagle County Airport, I got into my car and began driving back home—a place where I didn't want to be anymore without Ashley and Joy there. It was nearly ten o'clock, so traffic was light on I-70. I exited in Vail and kept my eyes on my rearview mirror. I'd noticed a black Ford Taurus pull out of the airport parking lot behind me. It had remained behind me on my entire drive down I-70. I wouldn't have thought too much of it except it was now exiting into Vail behind me. Coincidence? I couldn't be sure. It was impossible to see the driver through the glare of the headlights. I decided not to drive straight home and instead made a detour—just to see if the driver continued to trail me. They did. My heart started racing.

Who was it? Who was behind me?

I left Vail proper, made my way back under I-70 and up the road a bit to a well-lit gas station. I pulled up to a gas pump. I sat there a moment and watched my mirrors. The Ford Taurus pulled up to the curb just outside the entrance to the gas station, and the driver turned the headlights off. I couldn't get a good look from inside my vehicle, so I got out. I grabbed a gas nozzle and stuck it in my tank, even though I didn't need gas. I could now see across the parking lot and into the Ford Taurus. I cursed. Agent Chang was sitting in the driver's seat. Now my heart was really pumping. Who the hell was this guy? Had he been waiting for me to return from Laguna Beach? How had he even known I was there? My fear suddenly turned to anger. This was the same man who had gone into Ashley's hospital room the other night. And whatever had happened in there pushed her to run. He was the cause of all this.

I stepped away from the gas pump, began moving straight toward the Taurus. A swift walk quickly turned into an all-out charge. I could feel my muscles tighten. I wasn't sure what was about to happen, but I was ready for anything—even a physical encounter. I wanted answers. And I wanted them right now, no matter what it took. But Chang clearly wasn't interested in the same thing. The vehicle's headlights flashed on, and then the Taurus peeled away from the curb. I was sprinting now. Chang did a quick U-turn in the street. I met him there, pounding on the hood of the car.

"What do you want?" I yelled, staring at him through the windshield.

But I could tell Chang wasn't going to stop and chat, so I jumped out of the way before he floored it and raced off.

NINETEEN

I still felt jittery when I pulled my car into my garage. The encounter with Chang had my adrenaline steadily pumping. So many new questions were fighting for space in my already crowded head. Why had he been following me? How could he have known when my private plane was scheduled to land from California? Had someone also been following me around in Laguna Beach? I hadn't noticed anything suspicious. But I also hadn't been paying that much attention. I regretted that now. Could the guy I spoke with at the gallery have lied to me? Could he have made the call to Chang to alert him about me? I doubted it. I was usually a pretty good judge of character. That had helped me a lot in business. The guy at the gallery had seemed innocent as could be. And he certainly adored Ashley (or Amy).

I put my fingers to my temples and began massaging. I already had a pulsing headache, and this just added to it. But then I thought of a potential positive counterpoint. If Chang had been following me tonight, could that mean he didn't know where Ashley was? And he'd been hoping I would somehow lead him to her? I'd been carrying around a growing fear that Ashley and Joy had already been taken. That was why nobody out there had spotted them anywhere. And why

Ashley hadn't reached out to me. But instead, maybe she was hiding from this guy.

I got out of my car and dragged myself into the house. I was mentally and physically worn out. I pulled out my phone to call Danny and tell him what had just happened with Chang but then paused. I'd heard something down the hallway toward the primary bedroom. A banging noise. I stiffened, listened more intently. I heard it again. Someone was inside the house. I knew it wasn't Mark or Susan; I'd spoken to them earlier. Plus, all the lights were out.

Could it be Chang? It seemed unlikely that he'd race away from me at the gas station and then come straight over here. Could it be Ashley?

The last thought caused my feet to move quickly down the hallway before I could even think more about it. I paused again, listened. The noise was coming from my office. The door was cracked, and I could now see a light on inside the room. I carefully approached, my heart wanting to burst at the thought that Ashley might be inside. I found myself begging God. I slowly pushed the door open. It wasn't Ashley. It was a man in his twenties. I had a full moment to take him in before he noticed me. He was on his knees on the hardwood floor, searching through different items behind my desk. The guy had short spiky black hair and a goatee, and he wore earrings in both ears. He had on a military-green jacket and jeans. Who was he? And what should I do next?

But the guy determined that for me. He looked up, saw me watching him, and then charged right at me. He put his shoulder into my midsection and tackled me into the office wall. The impact took my breath away, but I managed to get my right arm wrapped around his head and tried to yank it back. He winced and hobbled backward. When he did, I launched myself at him. I hit him high, knocked him off his feet, and then landed square on top of him. We both grabbed on to each other, swinging wildly, trying to get the upper hand. I was bigger than him, but he was much quicker. He also seemed to know how to defend himself and easily blocked my punches.

But I was relentless. I could feel all my pent-up aggression coming out. He gave me a quick but solid punch to the jaw, and I saw stars for a moment. He was up and away from me. That's when I noticed a gun in a holster sticking out from beneath his jacket. But he never pulled it out. Instead, I saw him grab a small bag from the floor, and then he bolted for the hallway. I felt dizzy from the punch but tried to follow him. I staggered out into the hallway but wobbled a bit because my equilibrium was way off. I heard the front door open. I raced forward, getting there a couple of seconds later. The guy was sprinting up the driveway. I chased after him, unsure what I'd do if I actually caught him. The guy had a gun; I did not. But that didn't stop me. He took a left out of my driveway, rushed up the dark street in front of our house. He was faster than me, but I still pursued. I saw him jump into a gray Toyota Camry parked on the side of the street, slam the door shut, rev the engine. There was no way I would catch him now. So I stopped, squinted at the back license plate, and took a mental snapshot.

Then he was gone.

TWENTY

I went straight to the freezer, found an ice pack, and held it to my throbbing jaw. The stars were fading, and I was starting to regain my sensibilities. I had no clue who the guy was. I was certain I'd never seen him before. He had the rough look of a drug dealer or something like that. Had he robbed my house? Could it possibly have been random? Doubtful. The man had to be there for reasons connected to Ashley's situation—a situation that had now escalated beyond mystery and into more dangerous territory. My sore jaw was plenty proof of that. Then something flitted across my mind. I cursed, hustled up the hallway, and entered my office again. I kept a hidden safe in the bottom of the cabinets that lined the wall behind my desk. It was bolted all the way into the foundation of the home so no one could steal it. I stored critical business and personal papers in the safe. I also had $10,000 in cash. What I called an emergency fund.

I stepped around my desk. The lower cabinet door was open—and so was the safe. I knelt, stared inside, cursed again. The cash was gone. Everything else was still there. I carefully examined the safe door. Nothing looked tampered with. That likely meant the guy hadn't used a tool to somehow get the safe open—which would've been near impossible to do, anyway. He had to have used the code. My heart started racing. Only one person on the planet knew the code other than me: Ashley. So how had this guy gotten it? How had he known where we had the hidden safe? Could my wife have given him the code to come get the cash? It had been in the safe yesterday; I'd checked. So why wouldn't she have taken it when she'd first fled? Why send someone to get it now? Did she need it to run far away? Was that possible? If so, it opened a new realm of possibilities, all of which scared the hell out of me.

I stood, my mind racing, and moved around to the front of my desk. That's when I noticed a black bag the size of a small purse lying on the floor, right where I had wrestled with the guy. He must have dropped it during our fight. I bent down, picked it up, unzipped it. What I found inside hit me in the stomach as hard as the punch I'd just taken to the face. I sat in a guest chair, my legs feeling weak. I counted out four different driver's licenses. Each of them had a photo of Ashley. She had a variety of looks—blonde hair, brown hair, black hair, short hair, straight hair. Most of these were ones I'd never seen on her before. Each ID had a different name and addresses from across the country. I studied the ID from Laguna Beach first: Amy Sundown. Ashley was a blonde there, just like the guy from the art gallery had described. Kristin Bennett: Gatlinburg, Tennessee. Laura Hollings: Hudson, New York. Maggie Porter: Sedona, Arizona. How was this possible? How could Ashley have four different fake driver's licenses? Five, if I counted her current license. Had Ashley asked this guy to also retrieve this small purse from the house? Had she had it hidden somewhere? Even more, *why* did she have them all? Everything about the IDs looked completely authentic. In my estimation, a professional had to have put them together.

There were two other items inside the black bag: a piece of flowery card-stock stationery with a handwritten note on it and a glossy five-by-seven photograph. I read the note first.

Sarah,
I'm so proud of you. You have turned into such a beautiful young lady. I'm so grateful God brought us together. And I know he is going to use you to do something truly incredible. I will be praying for you on your trip and eagerly awaiting your return.
Love,
Janny

Sarah was not one of the names on any of the fake IDs. There was no date on the card, so I had no idea when it had been written. And who was Janny? I'd never heard any mention of her. I looked at the photograph. In it, Ashley was holding hands with an Asian man. They were both leaning into each other and smiling at the camera. It looked like they were standing in a garden somewhere. Ashley's hair was light brown and longer than I'd ever seen it. She was wearing a white sundress. She looked like she might be around twenty or so; I couldn't be sure. I did not recognize the man. He was probably late twenties, clean cut, black haired, wearing a white button-down shirt. Ashley was holding a bouquet of red roses in her other hand. They both looked happy. Could this man be Joy's real father? I flipped the photograph over, but nothing was written on the other side.

My head spinning, I walked behind my desk and sat in my office chair. Opening my laptop, I began searching Google for every name on the IDs. I found a lot of matches, but none of the photos appeared to look anything like Ashley. I checked each of the addresses listed. They were all real locations on real maps. I cross-checked the names with the cities listed: Sedona, Gatlinburg, Hudson. I got a hit in Sedona: a group photo of an art club posted three and a half years ago from someone's Facebook page. Eight women of all different ages were sitting on a patio bench somewhere. There were names listed for each woman, including Maggie Porter. I squinted. It was definitely Ashley, but her hair was black and much shorter. She was the only woman who was not really smiling in the photo. And the only person listed who was not tagged as having her own personal Facebook page.

I leaned back in my chair, short of breath. This was all real. Ashley really had lived as Maggie Porter in Sedona. That probably meant she'd also lived as Kristin Bennett in Gatlinburg, Tennessee, and Laura Hollings in Hudson, New York. I continued to dig. These locations were on opposite ends of the country. They were all small towns, with populations below ten thousand people. The towns were all known to have active art scenes. Was that why Ashley had chosen them? The dates on the driver's licenses all overlapped, so I had no idea when Ashley had lived in each place. Because of the date on the Facebook post of the art-club photo, I figured Sedona must've been right after she left Laguna Beach.

I rubbed my face in my hands, tried to go back over everything I'd unexpectedly discovered today. Ashley had lied about Joy's father. But she hadn't lied about living in Laguna Beach. A fake FBI agent seemed to be following me around—the same guy who had likely spooked Ashley into running in the first place. Someone had just been inside my house, clearly not expecting my inopportune arrival. He'd taken all the cash from the safe. And now I'd discovered Ashley had lived multiple lives.

I picked up my phone and called Danny Lamar with the FBI. I needed serious help. This had just exploded beyond anything I could've imagined.

"Agent Lamar," he answered, almost immediately.

"Danny, this is Luke Driskell."

"Oh, hey, man, how're you doing?"

"Not good. That's why I'm calling. Sorry if I woke you."

"Wake *me*?" He kind of laughed. "I'm still sitting at my desk at the office. I'm a night owl. Sometimes sleep here. What's up?"

I told him everything: My trip to Laguna Beach. My encounter at the gas station with Agent Chang. And my tussle with the guy in my office. Danny cursed in disbelief throughout my story. I couldn't believe it myself. How could any of it be real? A few nights ago, I'd been cuddled on the sofa with my new wife, wineglasses in our hands, watching the latest Ryan Reynolds movie. Life had felt so simple. So beautiful. But then, a tornado had struck. Danny asked me to take photos of all the IDs and text them over to him. He would also track the license plate of the Toyota Camry and see if that led anywhere. He would let me know more in the morning.

"Hang in there, man," Danny said to me.

"Should I also call the police?"

"Do you feel like you're still in danger?"

"I don't know what to think. I mean, this guy could've already shot me dead, but he didn't. So I think I'm okay."

"All right, good. Let me look into this first. The police have a way of unnecessarily complicating matters. I'll call you first thing in the morning."

I spent another hour searching the internet for any information I could find on Ashley's alternate identities in those other cities. I found a few more random listings here and there—mostly her various names connected to more art clubs, events, and so on—but no other photos. Ashley had clearly been very careful about being photographed before she ever came to Colorado. Of course, she hadn't been much of a fan of it ever since we'd been together. Why? That question stayed on repeat in my mind throughout the night.

Around midnight, I made the decision to go to these places to see for myself. My wife had just become a jigsaw puzzle, and I couldn't put all the pieces together from here in Vail. I jumped on the client portal for my private airline service to make arrangements for travel.

Exhausted, I tried lying down in my bed but felt uneasy being situated in the back of the house. I kept getting up and checking my front windows for any sign of a black Ford Taurus or a Toyota Camry. Would Agent Chang be visiting me again? Would the other guy come back for some reason? I wasn't sure. So I couldn't settle. I found myself sitting on my sofa, staring out my expansive glass front door.

The clock moved past one o'clock in the morning. Then two o'clock.

At some point, sleep finally won. But not for long.

My phone buzzing on the coffee table stirred me awake. I was going to ignore it, but then the thought of someone calling me or texting me at three in the morning woke me up a bit. I reached over, grabbed my phone. At first, I couldn't believe my eyes. Was I dreaming? It was a brief text message. On my screen was Ashley's photo—the one I had attached to her contact info in my phone. The name said Ashley Tolly. I had never changed her name to Driskell in my phone. I stared at the message in shock.

I'm sorry. I love you. Always.

This was real. Ashley had just texted me. My fingers shaking, I pressed on her phone number to call her. It went straight to her voice mail. I jumped up, started pacing, tried calling again. Same result. Had she turned her phone right back off? I scrambled to pull up my Find My app to see if I could grab her GPS location. My fingers were trembling so much I could barely work my phone. I cursed. There was no GPS signal. She must've sent the message and then immediately gone dark again.

I sat back down and typed out a quick reply.

I love you. You're safe with me. Please call me.

I hit Send. I kept reading her words. On one hand, it felt so damn good to finally hear *something* from her. Hopefully, the fact that she still had her phone with her meant she was somewhere safe. On the other hand, I couldn't stop staring at the word *Always*. It sent a cold shiver through me. Using that word didn't make me feel like Ashley was saying *I'll see you soon.*

It felt like she was saying goodbye.

TWENTY-ONE

I stared at my phone the rest of the night, not sleeping at all, desperately trying to will a response from Ashley. But nothing ever came. And no signal reappeared when I tried tracking her phone's GPS. I took a shower, got dressed in blue jeans and a dark-blue hoodie, and waited until seven in the morning to call Danny. But he didn't answer. I left a quick voice mail asking him to call me back ASAP. I'd been able to schedule a plane to pick me up at the Eagle airport around eight. I was hoping to speak with Danny before boarding to see what all he'd been able to discover, if anything.

I got in my Range Rover, left my house. I had a small bag with me—some extra clothes and toiletries. I had no idea what the day would bring and where it would take me. I wanted to be ready for anything. I decided to stop by the FBI branch on the way to the airport on the off chance Danny might be there, working. The guy had said he sometimes slept at the office. When I arrived, the dry cleaner, liquor store, and yoga studio that shared the same building strip were all still closed. The parking lot sat mostly empty. I did notice an older gray Ford Bronco with an SMU sticker on the back parked a few spots down from the FBI office's black-tinted front windows. Maybe Danny *was* here.

After parking next to the Bronco, I got out of my vehicle and walked up to the front door. I expected to find it locked, like it had been yesterday, so I was surprised when I was able to pull the door open. I poked my head inside. The lights were on in the office, but I didn't see anyone in the front room with the four desks. I also didn't hear anything.

"Danny? It's Luke Driskell."

No response. Maybe he was in the bathroom. I waited a minute or two near the front of the office, hoping he would appear from the back hallway. The last thing I wanted to do was walk back there and surprise a trained federal agent with a gun. I might get shot. But I got tired of waiting. I moved deeper into the room. I stared down at Danny's desk, where I'd sat with him the day before. The computer screens were all dark, as if he hadn't recently been logged on. Could he have possibly left his office last night without turning the lights off and locking the front door?

I moved toward the back hallway. "Danny, you back here?"

Nothing. I decided to make a full sweep before leaving. The guy could have headphones on or something. When I turned the next corner into a small kitchen, I stiffened, feeling a rush of horror push me up against the wall. Danny was lying on his back on the cheap tile floor, arms and legs splayed out. His eyes were open, but he wasn't moving—because there was a hole the size of a quarter in the middle of his forehead. Dried blood had pooled down out of the hole on both sides of his face. There was also a puddle of dried blood beneath him on the kitchen floor. My stomach flipped over at the sight of the body, the hole, the blood, threatening to spew up the protein bar I'd eaten a few minutes ago.

For a second, I could hardly think or process any of it. I tried to take several breaths, to calm down, but it was extremely difficult. Danny was dead. Someone had shot him in the office. I could now see some dark streaks on the floor around me and up the hallway toward the main office. They must've shot him out there in the main room and then dragged him back in here. I presumed it had occurred much earlier in the night. The blood had dried, and his computer screens were all dark. The next question that popped into my head scared the hell out of me: Could it have been connected to our phone call? Had Danny been shot and killed because he was looking into that guy from last night?

Again, my stomach threatened to empty. I had to get the hell out of there immediately. Whoever had done this to Danny could still be close by. They could be outside, watching the office. They could be coming in with a gun at any moment. I spun around, hurried from the back hallway. I stopped by Danny's desk, where I spotted printouts of Ashley's fake IDs sticking out from a folder. I opened the folder, quickly skimmed them all—there didn't seem to be any new information—but then I paused on a printout at the bottom of the stack. It was from a Hertz Rental Car agreement for a Toyota Camry rented at Denver International two days ago. Nick Cantley. Was this the guy from last night? I got my answer on another printout clipped behind the car-rental agreement. This one had a profile picture of the guy who had been in my house. It looked like an official government document. The information listed beside the photo stunned me. Nick Cantley: Falls Church, Virginia. *Central Intelligence Agency, United States of America.* A date range was listed. Cantley had worked for the CIA for eight years, up until four years ago, at least according to this printout. I felt a chill race through me. Why would a former CIA agent break into my house and steal ten thousand in cash? How was he connected with Ashley? What the hell was going on?

I didn't have time to stand there and process it. I folded the printout, stuffed it in my back pocket, and headed for the front door. I took a moment to peek out before stepping outside. I scanned back and forth; I didn't see anyone watching. There were two other cars in the parking lot: a red Acura parked in front of the liquor store and a white Jeep Wrangler that sat way across on the other side. I couldn't see anyone inside either of the vehicles.

I stepped outside, rushed over to my Range Rover, and climbed inside. Every part of me was shaking. I sat there a moment, trying to sort out what to do next. I couldn't believe Danny was dead. Should I call the police? Or call the main FBI office in Denver? I knew if I did, my search plans for the day would be done. I'd likely spend all day with the authorities, going over everything that had happened. I blew out hard between my lips. I couldn't do that right now. I couldn't forfeit my chance of possibly finding Ashley today. I felt like I was getting closer to answers. Her text message to me last night had brought on a fresh wave of hope that this could still be resolved. I had to keep hunting for the truth. I had to keep searching for Ashley and Joy.

But what would happen if I didn't make the call about Danny? How long would it take for someone else to find the body? Hours? An entire day? When someone eventually did, would the police somehow suspect me? Were there security cameras inside the FBI office? I looked up and down the front of the retail strip. I didn't spot any security cameras outside the other stores. There probably weren't any; this was not a high-end shopping strip. Even if I made the call to the police or the FBI, whom could I trust? I'd already been fooled once by a fake FBI agent. And now a real one had been shot dead only hours after I had called him to investigate a former CIA agent who had been inside my home. I quickly backed out of my parking spot, punched on the gas, and sped toward the airport.

I decided I couldn't trust anyone. Not right now.

TWENTY-TWO

I don't think I took a full breath until my plane was finally up in the air. I kept fearing an unexpected encounter with whomever had killed Danny. My mind kept flashing on the image of the FBI agent lying there on the kitchen floor. The bullet hole was dead center of his forehead. That led me to believe it was the work of a professional. Someone who was an excellent marksman. Was it Nick Cantley, the former CIA agent? I wasn't convinced. The guy had had an opportunity to shoot me but didn't. So why would he drive over to the FBI office and kill Danny? Plus, he probably wouldn't have left behind the printouts about himself. Could it have been Chang, whose real identity I still didn't know? Or could it possibly be unrelated to my situation?

There was no way for me to know the truth. I just had to keep going. I had to focus on the task at hand: finding out answers about Ashley that would hopefully lead me to bringing her and Joy safely home. Along with my laptop, I had each of Ashley's fake IDs pulled out on the table in front of me. It still felt impossible for me to wrap my mind around the fact that my wife had apparently lived as five different people over the last four years. And in places that were spread across the US map. She had to be hiding from something—or someone.

Who was Joy's real father? The mystery guy in the photograph with her?

And was that still central to this entire ordeal?

I picked up the ID from Sedona, Arizona, where I was currently headed. Maggie Porter. Her hair was dark black, straight, and much shorter than it was today. She barely looked like my Ashley, except for those inimitable eyes. The birth date was even different from the one I knew. I again wondered who had secured this ID for her. How would Ashley even have that kind of contact? Could she possibly be connected to the CIA?

That thought seemed completely preposterous. I'd seen nothing from her over the past year that would even remotely make me believe that. Because I worked from home, we were rarely apart. I would know if there was something more to her life.

Or would I?

I sat back in my chair, stared out the window as we soared high above the clouds, thinking about Sedona. I'd been there recently, back in February. I'd had a meeting with the head of another tech firm who had a big house there. He had wanted me to bring Ashley so he and his wife could wine and dine us. But Ashley had rebuffed the offer, even with my pleading.

"I don't understand," I said. "We can take Joy with us if you want."

"It's not that," Ashley said.

I was standing at my kitchen island while she made a pasta dish at the stove top. Joy was in the living room, playing with dolls. Ashley and I had been dating more seriously the past few months. There was something that felt natural about the way we fit together. I knew it was because money was not the center of our relationship. That was something I'd never really had with Jill. While I loved my former wife, I think I initially moved toward her because it felt like she fit with my dream for my life. Jill was from a wealthy family. She was used to nice things. She dressed in the latest fashions, and we always were the best-looking couple at events and parties. But if I was honest with myself, it always felt a bit forced between us. Like I was making it happen more out of an image I wanted to portray to the world and not the intricate workings of my own heart. I don't think I fully realized that until I met and spent this time with Ashley. While we operated in different worlds, I felt like our roots deeply bonded us. I liked being able to talk to her about my poor childhood. There were so many stories to share, good and bad. I'd been so reserved with Jill out of fear of being judged and rejected, even after we were married. But I felt free with Ashley. She not only accepted but embraced the poor kid from Texas. I was already desperately in love with her. I'd even been thinking about rings lately. That's how serious I was about our future together.

"Is it the fear-of-flying thing?" I asked. "Because I'll drive us if you want. I think it's only nine hours from here. It could be a fun road trip."

She dismissed that suggestion. "I'm just busy, Luke."

"But you just turned in your latest painting."

"And I would like to get a jump start on my next one. It's commissioned."

"Come on, Ashley. It's only two days. Plus, Sedona is known for its art. We could spend half our time there in galleries."

I saw a flash of something hit her eyes. "I don't want to go."

"Ashley, please. It will be fun."

She set her narrowed eyes on me now. "No, okay? Just stop already!"

I was surprised by her firm tone. I hadn't heard it before. She then pulled off the black apron she'd been wearing and set it on top of the island.

"I think I need to go," she announced.

"Hey," I said, reaching for her. "Don't go. I'll drop it. No big deal."

She sighed. "I'm just really tired tonight. I shouldn't have come over."

"Ashley, please stay. I'll take over the cooking."

She paused. I could suddenly see tears in her eyes. "I'm not sure I can do this, Luke."

I tilted my head. "Do what?"

She looked at me. "This. Us."

That hit me hard. "I don't understand. Things are going great with us."

"I know, it's just . . ." She hesitated.

"Just what? Tell me."

"I'm scared."

"Scared of what?"

She took a long moment. "I just need some sleep, that's all."

I stared back down at her Sedona driver's license. Ashley hadn't wanted to go to Sedona with me because she'd lived there. People might recognize her and call her Maggie—especially if we went into the galleries. She didn't want me to know anything about her past. About any of this. Was she ever going to tell me? There had been so many times over the past year when it had seemed like Ashley wanted to tell me something important but didn't.

I was hoping Sedona would give me a clue as to why.

TWENTY-THREE

The plane landed at the tiny Sedona airport. I climbed down the short stairs to the tarmac. The pilot would be waiting for my return; I had booked the plane for basically the entire day. I found my way inside the small and fairly empty terminal. The airport was not for commercial flights but only for smaller planes and private jets like mine. I took a quick look around. I felt confident no one could have followed me from Vail—not when I was on a private flight—but I'd wondered if I'd find anyone waiting for me here. I had no idea who I was looking for, of course. I hadn't noticed anyone giving me any second glances.

After pulling out my phone, I used my Uber app to request a ride. It took about five minutes before a white Ford Explorer pulled up to the curb outside the terminal. I quickly hopped inside. As I rode in the back into Sedona proper—about an eight-minute drive—I scrolled through texts and checked voice mails. Both the detective with Vail police and Doug Pederson had called that morning and left messages. I didn't feel like calling either one of them back at the moment. I no longer believed they could provide anything helpful for me. This thing had gone beyond them. And I didn't want to misstep and possibly lie about what had happened over the past twelve hours or so. I felt committed to doing this on my own now. I believed it was the only way forward.

I'd given my Uber driver—a quiet guy with thick glasses—the address on Ashley's fake ID. I'd already done my research online. The place at this address looked like a typical tan stucco Santa Fe–style town house near the town's center. My driver pulled up to it a few minutes later. The one-story structure was surrounded by a dozen others that all looked the same. I offered the driver two hundred in cash if he'd stay with me around town the next couple of hours—or for however long this took. I was flying a bit blind here, as far as any real plan. I just knew I needed to come here first, where Ashley had supposedly lived, and then start sorting out what to do next. I walked up to the stucco unit. The place was small, couldn't be more than two bedrooms. Had Ashley really lived here? Or was it just an address she'd used on the ID? I needed to find that out. I looked over and noticed a Realtor sign was stuck in the rock bed near the front walk: COMING SOON.

I made a call to the number on the sign.

"Marissa Gomez," a woman answered.

It was the same name the sign listed. "Hi, Marissa, I wanted to get some information about the place on Verde Valley School Road."

"Great. That's a beautiful place. Newly remodeled inside. Upgraded appliances. The works."

"How long has the seller owned it?"

"Ten years. It's been a rental property for him."

That was good news. Ashley would've likely rented. And that would mean she'd have rented from the same guy who was now selling the unit.

"Is he local?" I asked.

"Yes. A longtime resident of Sedona."

"I'd like to speak with him. I'm also interested in using it for a rental property and wanted to ask him some detailed questions."

"Do you want to take a look inside first?"

"That's not necessary. I already love it. Perfect location."

"It is. Easy walking distance to lots of shops and restaurants. Is this the best number to reach you?"

"Yes."

"Okay, let me call him."

I hung up and started to circle the block, wondering if any of the neighbors would've been here at the same time as Ashley. I was willing to knock on doors to find out. My phone buzzed. It was a different Sedona phone number from the one I'd just called for the Realtor.

"Jack Mackey," he said. "You interested in my place?"

"Possibly. Thanks for calling. Any chance we can meet in person?"

"I, uh, guess. Is that necessary?"

"I'm a cash buyer, Jack. And I prefer to look someone in the eye when doing a transaction of this magnitude."

I hoped the mention of a cash offer would be enticing enough.

"I hear ya. Yeah, sure. I got some time this morning."

He gave me his address. I hurried back to my Uber driver, climbed inside, and gave him the new address. Five minutes later, he pulled up in front of a charming old world–style hacienda located on top of a hill. There was a lush outdoor-patio area on the side of the house overlooking a canyon of red rocks. I walked up a xeriscape path to the front door and knocked. A skinny older man with a neatly trimmed red-and-gray beard answered, wearing casual surfer shorts and a white tank top. He looked like he belonged on the beach somewhere.

"Jack?" I asked.

"Yes, sir. Wade?"

"Yep. Thanks for letting me stop over."

I hadn't wanted to use my real name. I had no idea who might come right behind me asking questions. I was playing my own shadow game now.

"No problemo." He stepped out, shut the door behind him. "It's a beautiful morning. Let's chat over here on the patio." He held up a glass. "You want something to drink? I make a mean Bloody Mary."

"No, I'm good. Thank you."

I followed him down a path to the outdoor-patio area on the side of the house, where we sat in two red Adirondack chairs.

"Quite the view," I mentioned.

"Yeah. Bought this place twenty years ago, and I'll never leave because of the view. You should see the sunset. It'll knock your socks off."

"I bet."

"So what would you like to know about the town house?" he asked.

"How many renters have you had in there?"

"Well, I've had the place ten years. So probably a dozen or so."

"You remember them all?"

"Probably not. I have a lot of rental places around town."

I pulled out Ashley's Sedona ID. "Do you remember her?"

He leaned forward, studied the photo. "Absolutely."

"Why do you say it like that?"

"Well, for one, she was a real looker. But she also broke her lease by disappearing on me overnight."

"Really?"

He cocked his head at me. "You're not looking to buy, are you?"

"Honestly, no. Sorry. But I really wanted to talk to you."

"About her?"

"Yes."

"Why?"

He didn't seem to be too annoyed at me being there under false pretenses. I'd been concerned he might shut things down the moment he realized I wasn't an actual buyer. But there was something casually cool about Jack. I doubted he was bothered by much. Not with that Bloody Mary in his hand.

"She's my sister," I lied. "And she's missing."

"Wow. I'm sorry to hear that."

"I think it might somehow be related to when she lived here in Sedona. So I was hoping you could tell me whatever you remember about her."

He blew air out forcefully. "I mean, I'll try. But my mind isn't what it used to be anymore. That was nearly four years ago, I think. Maggie wasn't here too long. Maybe three months. She was pregnant at the time."

I thought about that. Ashley had probably come here to Sedona right after abruptly leaving Laguna Beach. It was the closest to California.

"She wanted to pay cash," Jack continued. "I don't usually do cash, but she sweet-talked me into it. Told me her credit was shot."

"Did she have her baby while living here?"

He shook his head. "No, she left well before that."

"You said she disappeared overnight?"

He took a long drink of his Bloody Mary. "Yeah. It was so strange, I tell you. I came by one afternoon to fix a leak in her kitchen faucet while she was out. I remember Maggie came home while I was still there working on it. She seemed fine—pleasant and sweet. Just like always. I told her I needed to get another part and would be by first thing the next morning to finish the job. When I showed up the next day, she was gone. Her closet and bathroom were completely cleaned out. I tried to call her for several days, but her number was no longer working. So I gave up. I've wondered a few times over the past couple of years whatever happened to her." Another sip of his drink. "Like I said, sweet gal."

I thought about that. What could have made Ashley disappear so abruptly—just like she had in Laguna Beach? What had chased her out of Sedona?

"Was Maggie close to anyone else around town that you know about?"

"Can't say. I was just her landlord. I only talked with her once or twice a week when issues came up. But I know she had the attention of the young men in town. I owned another unit in that same complex. Two young guys who lived there were always asking me about her." He kind of laughed. "My painter even asked about her. As a matter of fact, a young man showed up looking for her the day I was fixing her faucet."

This made me sit up. "Someone you knew?"

"No, I didn't know him."

"What did the guy say?"

"Not much. He was just looking for Maggie."

"You remember what he looked like?"

"You're really making me think hard, aren't you?" He took another deep breath and let it out slowly, staring off into the red rocks. "Let's see. He was probably around your age, I suppose. Asian guy. Clean cut. No facial hair. Dressed nicely, if I remember correctly."

I pulled out the five-by-seven photograph of Ashley with the mystery man.

"Was this the guy?" I asked him.

Jack took the photograph, examined it. "Nah, it wasn't him."

My mind then went to Chang. Could he have possibly been here in Sedona, looking for Ashley nearly four years ago? I pulled out my phone, brought up the hospital security photo, and showed it to Jack.

"How about this guy?" I asked.

Jack leaned in, squinted, and took a moment. "Yeah, I think that's him."

I felt my heart pick up two beats. "Did you tell Maggie about him?"

He nodded. "Yes, I did. When she came home that day."

"Did she seem concerned?"

"Not that I recall." His eyes narrowed. "Who is he?"

"I'm not sure. But he could be the reason she left town so quickly."

TWENTY-FOUR

I made several other stops around Sedona before getting back on the plane. I popped into a long list of art galleries, showing them Maggie Porter's ID, asking if anyone remembered her. Several did but couldn't offer me much else about her. It didn't seem like Ashley had attached herself too closely to anyplace in particular, like she'd done in Laguna Beach. Most of what I got was that she was a nice young lady who had come to different shows and events. But no one seemed to have gotten to know her very well. And no one knew if she had a job anywhere. From what I gathered, Ashley had come to Sedona after Laguna Beach and spent nearly four months here, according to Jack's official records. Jack had said she was probably two months away from having her child when she'd left town. And she'd split only hours after Chang had come around asking about her—the same way she'd vanished immediately after Chang had come to see her at the hospital in Vail.

The same questions kept ping-ponging in my head.

Who the hell was Chang? Why was he searching for Ashley?

Who had helped Ashley relocate with the new IDs?

And was all this about Joy?

My thoughts focused in on my precious and innocent stepdaughter. She had to be at the center of all this. I pulled out my cell phone, began scrolling through photos. I had a whole album dedicated to just Joy. She was smiling so big in nearly every single photo. That smile—it slayed me every single time. I couldn't resist it. I thought about one particular smile that would stay with me forever.

"Higher, higher," Joy said, gripping the chains on the swing tightly.

"Are you sure?" I replied. "You're getting really high already."

"Higher, higher," she repeated.

"Okay, here goes." I gave her a big push.

She squealed with absolute delight as the swing carried her toward the sky. We were at the Pirate Ship Playground, Joy's favorite park. She loved to climb up to the top of the ship and make pirate noises. Joy was fearless. It was the day after Ashley told me she would marry me. We had not yet informed Joy about it. I asked Ashley if I could do it myself. I needed to ask this little girl if it would be okay if I married her mother. I had to admit, I was kind of nervous.

I finally managed to get her off the swing set.

"Can I talk to you for a moment, Joy?" I asked.

"More pirate ship first!"

She probably thought I was trying to get her to leave. "We can stay and play on the pirate ship for as long as you want. But I need to ask you something first."

"Okay."

I knelt in front of her and held her tiny hands in mine. "You know I love you, right, sweetheart?"

She nodded. "Me, too!"

I smiled. "And I love your mommy so much, too."

"Mommy and Luke, sitting in a tree—" she said, swaying to music in her mind. She had been singing this ever since she'd caught us kissing for the first time.

"Right. Something like that. Would you be okay if I married your mom?"

Her mouth popped open. "Really?"

"Yes, really."

She looked down at the ground. I could see her little mind trying to process this. Then she looked up at me. "Would you be my daddy?"

"Yes, I would."

Tears immediately hit her eyes. "Really?" she asked again, as if what I'd said the first time couldn't possibly be true. Big eye puddles were forming.

My eyes were also now wet. "Yes, I mean it."

She smiled ear to ear, wiping her wet face with her fingers. But then she looked at me more seriously. "Would you ever leave?"

"Never. I will always be here for you. I promise."

Again, her face lit up. She lunged at me. I pulled her in tight, trying not to squeeze her too hard. The night before, when Ashley had said yes to my proposal, I'd felt something electric move through my entire being. I felt something equal but altogether different holding Joy now. Love, yes. But more than that. Something fierce in my soul. I knew right then I would do anything from this point forward to protect this child. My child.

I put my phone down and took a deep breath, trying to push back the tears as I stared out the plane window. I had made a promise to Joy, but I had failed to keep it. She had to be so scared and confused wherever she was. Was she safe? What was Ashley telling her? How was she explaining to my stepdaughter why I wasn't there with them? I thought about the text from Ashley. I'm sorry. I love you. Always. I couldn't help but imagine Ashley telling Joy that she would never see me again.

That's when the dam broke, and I sobbed.

TWENTY-FIVE

The plane landed early afternoon at Gatlinburg Pigeon Forge Airport, about a dozen miles outside the town of Gatlinburg, where Ashley had been Kristin Bennett. I couldn't wrap my mind around how Ashley had somehow ended up in this remote mountain town in East Tennessee with a population of just under four thousand people. Had she known someone here? Had she done her research? Or had she just kept driving across the country until a place looked safe and inviting to her? I had two remaining fake IDs: Gatlinburg and Hudson, New York. I didn't yet know which place Ashley had moved after bolting from Sedona. My guess was Tennessee. While Gatlinburg was nearly two thousand miles from Sedona, Hudson was more than 2,500 miles. I tried to imagine my wife, at seven months pregnant, driving across America to set up a new life in some random small town. How does one even start all over with a brand-new name? Does it take very long to get used to it? When people said her new name, would she forget to look?

This time I booked a rental car online while on the plane and found a simple black Chevrolet Malibu waiting for me at the airport. I drove north to Gatlinburg, which was a beautiful town known as the gateway to the Great Smoky Mountains National Park. The only real guess I had on how Ashley had somehow ended up here was that the small town had a vibrant art scene, according to Google. So did Hudson.

My GPS map led me to an older 1960s ranch-style home with a large screened-in front porch isolated off Tank Hill Road. I pulled off the main road and onto the grass shoulder. The house probably had three or four bedrooms, so I doubted Ashley had lived here by herself. Maybe someone was renting out rooms. I pulled up toward the cracked driveway. The house didn't look like much: faded, aged, leaning in places. But it was placed in a fantastic wooded setting, as were all the homes I'd passed by on this street. I could tell there was much to like about living in Gatlinburg.

I got out of my rental, walked up to the house. There was a white Jeep Cherokee parked in the driveway with an orange Tennessee Volunteers bumper sticker. I had to step inside the screened-in porch to knock on the front door. I could hear some rumbling around going on inside, so I knew someone was home. A lady, probably in her fifties, with fiery-red hair answered the door. She wore a gray sweatshirt with *Go Vols* on the front and blue jeans. I could see that her fingernails were also painted bright orange.

"Good afternoon—" I said, before getting cut off.

"I ain't buying nothing."

I smiled. "Well, I'm not selling anything."

"Then what do you want?"

I could tell this was a no-nonsense woman, so I got straight to it. I held up the fake driver's license for Kristin Bennett, who had short blonde hair in the photo. She looked so different from the woman I'd married.

"I'm looking for my sister," I said.

She stepped forward, squinted at the ID. "Yeah, I know Kristin. Or I *knew* her. But that was a good while back."

"She lived here?"

"For a brief time. I sometimes rent a bedroom when I need some extra cash."

"Can you tell me when she was here?"

She eyeballed me. "She in some kind of trouble?"

"She went missing a few days ago."

"Oh dear." This softened her tone. "What happened?"

"Long story, but I'm trying to retrace some of her steps the last few years because I think it could help me find her."

"Well, she was here probably three years ago. Stayed with me about four months, I think. But I haven't seen or spoken with her since she left. Which was rather abruptly."

"How do you mean?"

The woman shrugged. "She just came home one day, packed up her things, said she had to go."

"Was she acting strange?"

"Yeah, panicked. I tried to get her to slow down. I was concerned about her baby. I thought how hard it would be for her to just uproot like that with a newborn."

"She had her baby while living with you?"

"Yep. I drove her to the dang hospital myself."

I was right: Ashley must've come straight here from Sedona. "How old was the baby when she left?"

"Not even two months. And Kristin didn't seem to have much money to take care of her. I felt sorry for her. I gave her whatever cash I had on me so she could buy diapers and whatever. She told me she didn't have any family, so I had no idea she had a brother."

"We were estranged. Did anyone come by your place looking for her before or after she left?"

"What? Like the cops?"

"Or a stranger."

She shook her head. "Can't recall."

I pulled out my phone and showed her the image of Chang. "Did you ever see him around here while she lived with you?"

She again shook her head. "Nope."

I then showed her the five-by-seven photograph. "How about him?"

"Don't recognize him, either. I don't think any guy ever came here."

"Did Ashley leave anything behind?"

She squinted at me. "Who?"

I realized my mistake. "I mean, Kristin. Did Kristin leave anything behind?"

"No." She gave me a crooked smile. "Just dirty diapers."

I smiled back. I felt grateful for this woman. She'd been there for Ashley and Joy at a critical time. "Thank you for helping her out while she was here."

"Of course. She was the sweetest gal. Very quiet. Kept mostly to herself and stayed in her bedroom. But she had the cutest baby I think I've ever seen in my life. I loved holding that sweet pea. I was real sorry to see them both go. Hadn't had a baby in my house in years. My kids are grown, but none of them have given me a grandchild yet."

"Do you want to see a picture of her little girl now?" I offered.

Her eyes sparked up. "Yes, please."

I pulled out my phone, showed her several photos of Joy.

"Oh my dear," she said. "Janny sure did turn into an angel."

I tried to hide my surprise. My stepdaughter hadn't always been Joy. Ashley had also changed her name. That revelation hit me hard. Maybe even harder than discovering Ashley's different names. Janny. I thought about the name. It was the same name I'd found scribbled at the bottom of the handwritten letter inside the black bag with Ashley's fake IDs. Had Ashley originally named Joy after this person? If so, she must've been important to her. Who was she?

I sighed, not sure where to go next. But then I thought of something. "Where did Kristin deliver her baby?"

"Over at LeConte Medical Center."

TWENTY-SIX

LeConte Medical Center was in Sevierville, twenty minutes up the road from Gatlinburg. It was a nice earth-toned brick-and-stone building. I parked in the visitor lot out front and walked inside. The maternity center was called the Dolly Parton Birthing Unit. I took an elevator up to the second level and found myself standing in front of a reception desk with a silver-haired woman wearing readers who already had a serious scowl on her face.

She peered up at me over her glasses. "Can I help you?"

Her southern twang was thick. "Gretchen" was on her name tag.

I gave her my most charming smile. "I hope so, Gretchen. I need to get medical records from when my wife gave birth here."

She stared down at her computer. "Name?"

"Kristin Bennett."

She pecked away on her keyboard, stared at her screen. "June second? Three years ago?"

I nodded. Ashley had not changed Joy's date of birth. I found some comfort in that. I wanted to find as many things as possible that remained true to what I knew about both.

"Can I see some ID?" Gretchen asked.

I knew this part was where it was going to get tricky. I pulled out my driver's license and handed it over.

She squinted at it, looked at me. "Different last names?"

"Right. We married recently."

"So you're not the father of the child who was born here?"

"Correct. I'm not."

She handed my ID back. "I'm sorry, sir, but I can't give you access to anything without your wife's authorization."

"I understand that. But she's not available."

"Then you need to come back when she is available."

This was not going well. The woman was an iron wall.

"Listen, Gretchen, this is an emergency. My wife—"

"Sorry, sir. Policy is policy."

"But you don't understand—"

"Sir, I've worked in medical care for over forty years and have never once broken policy. And it isn't happening today."

I sighed, my shoulders sagging. But Gretchen was unmoved by my clear exasperation. She looked away from me and started vigorously typing on her keyboard again.

I turned and walked back toward the elevators, but there was no way I was simply going to get in my rental car and drive away. If a hospital administrator wasn't going to volunteer the information I needed, I would have to find another way to access it. I glanced over my shoulder, noticed Gretchen eyeballing me a bit over her glasses. I pulled my phone out and pretended to have a conversation. She finally got busy doing something else. Glancing over to my left, I spotted a hallway leading back to the maternity wing. The door was secure, but a steady stream of people—medical staff and guests—was going in and out. I gave one more glance at Gretchen, who was no longer watching me, and then walked briskly toward the hallway.

I followed a father with two young boys holding pink balloons that said Baby Girl! on them through the door. Maternity rooms lined the exterior of the hallway, with medical desks, counters, and offices on the inside. It was quite busy. Various doctors and nurses were darting all about. I saw a nurse behind a counter look up at me while I was just standing there, so I smiled and got moving like I knew where I was going. I clocked the room numbers on each door as I passed by them and tried to monitor the nurse stations out of my peripheral vision. I needed access to a computer. If I could get sixty seconds on one, I could probably find what I wanted. But that would be no easy task. Medical staff was everywhere. I kept slowly walking, circling the entire floor, smiling as I passed by others in the hallway, looking for an opportunity. I finally found an opening. Two nurses were working on computers behind a counter, and they both got up at the same time to go address something around the corner. Their area was empty, and they were not in sight.

I slipped into one of the chairs—the one with my back to the hallway—and put my fingers on the keyboard. The computer was already logged into their system. Someone's medical records were currently on the screen. I could feel my heart racing. What kind of trouble could I get into if I got caught doing this? I found a search box near the top right of the screen. I typed in *Kristin Bennett* and the exact date of Joy's (Janny's) birth. Her medical record popped right onto the screen. The hallway was buzzing with activity behind me, but I never turned to look around. I couldn't waste a single second. It was straightforward medical information. Ashley's height, weight, and other measurements were listed. I squinted at the screen, searching for the father's name. I cursed. It was blank. No father listed. I scrolled down the page to see if there was anything else that might help me. There was an official timeline of Janny's birth. Then baby measurements. I kept scrolling down and found a scanned document attached to her digital file. It was a simple fake birth certificate that I presumed hospitals gave out to parents as a keepsake to take home for scrapbooks. Each of the blanks had been filled in with what I clearly recognized as Ashley's handwriting. Very neat with an artistic flair to it. Janny, not Joy. Born June 2. Six pounds, seven ounces. Nineteen inches. Mother: Kristin Bennett. Father: Han Liu.

This made me perk up. Ashley had written the father's name on her own document. Han Liu? It meant nothing to me in the moment. But I had a gut feeling that finally finding out the truth about my wife might mean everything to me—and hopefully that truth would lead me to bringing her safely home.

"Sir, what are you doing?"

A woman's voice, coming from behind and clearly speaking to me. It was time to bolt. I spun around, found the same nurse I'd spotted sitting in this seat a moment ago. She did not look pleased to see me at her desk. I quickly got up.

"Sorry, I was just trying to google restaurants that deliver here," I said.

She stared down at the screen. Clearly I was not on Google. Ashley's file was still on the screen. She looked back up at me, her brow furrowed. I didn't have another good explanation, so I just brushed past her without another word. I didn't look back, but I heard her grab a phone and say, "I need security ASAP."

That sent a chill through me. I picked up the pace, turned a corner. How close by was security? I found my answer when I spotted a man in a black security uniform enter the hallway through the secure doors. I stopped in my tracks, glanced to my left. A door to a maternity room was open. I slipped inside. A family was gathered around a woman in bed, who held a baby. They all stopped what they were doing and looked over at me.

I tried to think fast, put up an apologetic hand. "So sorry—wrong room. I keep getting lost in here. And I'm so tired from last night's birth that I can't even think straight."

An elderly woman smiled. "Believe us, we understand. What did you have?"

I had one eye out the door on the hallway. The security guard hurried past.

"What's that?" I muttered, not really paying attention.

"Did you have a boy or a girl?" the woman asked me.

I smiled. "Both. Twins."

Then I jetted out as they were all saying congratulations. I took a quick peek to my right. The guard was already thirty feet past me. I rushed toward the door out of the maternity wing. On my way, I spotted an empty chair behind a desk with a black sweater jacket wrapped over the back. Barely slowing, I snagged it, tucked it under my arm, and hoped no one noticed. I hit the doorway out to the second-floor lobby. Pausing briefly, I pulled the black sweater on over my hoodie. It was tight but it fit okay. I zipped it all the way up to my neck. I was sure the nurse would tell security to look for a guy in a dark-blue hoodie. I hoped I'd just stolen myself some cover. I glanced over to the reception desk and noticed Gretchen standing there, staring at me with narrowed eyes. Had she seen me just come from the maternity wing? Did she notice I now had on a black sweater?

Trying to be casual, I smiled, waved. But she didn't smile back.

Even though everything within me wanted to run for it, I walked slowly toward the elevators. I couldn't fathom the thought of getting apprehended by hospital security right now and it somehow putting an end to my day's search. Especially when I finally had a name for Joy's father. A name I was desperate to put into a Google search. I chose the stairs instead of the elevator, pushed through a door, and since no one else was inside the stairwell, bounded down three steps at a time. I was sweating profusely. I pushed open a door to the ground floor, paused to make sure the coast was clear, and then stepped out into another lobby. I nearly froze when a second security guard appeared from around the corner. He was searching the faces passing through the lobby. Had he been alerted to the activity upstairs? I had to presume so.

I was a sitting duck with nowhere to turn and hide. So I swallowed, stuck my hands in my pockets, and walked toward him. He pivoted and looked straight at me.

I forced a smile, said, "How're you doing?"

He gave me a brief nod. "Good."

Then his eyes moved on from me. I kept walking at a steady pace toward the main exit of the hospital. I was only twenty feet away. Almost there. Ten feet. Five feet. Then I heard a man's voice booming from somewhere behind me.

"Sir, can you hold up a second?"

He had to be talking to me. The only other people near the exit right now were two women. Was it the same security guard I had just passed? I couldn't risk turning to find out. I was only a couple of feet from the exit. I picked up my pace, hurried out the sliding glass doors. I heard the same voice again.

"Sir!"

I was done walking; it was time to run. I took off at full speed toward the main parking lot, ducking low while zigzagging through the cars, catching a few odd glances from others. I found my rental car where I'd left it, quickly unlocked it, and jumped inside. Through my windshield, I could see the same security guard standing on the sidewalk, scanning the parking lot. He had not noticed where I'd gone. I started my car, pulled out of my parking spot, and turned down the aisle. The guard hopped off the sidewalk, began walking into the main parking lot, his eyes bouncing all around. There were probably a dozen other cars coming and going. The guard was making a path through the rows right in front of where I was headed. I needed to get out in front of him. So I stepped on the gas a little harder and sped up. This meant cutting off someone who was trying to back out. The guard was within fifteen feet of me now. I sank a little lower in my seat, sped up a little bit more. My rental car zipped by the guard, who stepped out into my aisle right behind me. He was looking in the other direction.

I found the exit lane, pulled into it, and finally took a breath.

I had made it out.

TWENTY-SEVEN

I sat in my rental car in the parking lot down the street from the hospital and immediately began researching the name Han Liu on my phone. A lot of hits started popping up on my first entry into Google. A professor at Stanford. A geophysicist in Chicago. A research scientist at Boston College. A tax accountant in Miami. An investment banker in New York City. And so many more. It was a popular Chinese name. How was I supposed to find out which of these guys, if any, was Joy's father? I began grouping searches together: *Han Liu* and *Kristin Bennett*; *Han Liu* and *Amy Sundown*; *Han Liu* and *Maggie Porter*; *Han Liu* and *Laura Hollings*; *Han Liu* and *Ashley Tolly*. I scrolled for pages and pages but found nothing that clearly tied any of these full names together. I tried grouping Han Liu with the name Nick Cantley, the former CIA agent who'd been in my home. Nothing. I typed in the name Kai Lin, the art-gallery owner Ashley had known in Laguna Beach, and tagged it with Han Liu.

This time I got something. And it jarred me.

It was a snippet of a profile article from *Laguna Beach Magazine* written five years ago, when Kai Lin had first opened his new art gallery. Lin still has prominent roots back in his homeland of China. He is the nephew of Chen Liu, the current Chinese ambassador to the United

States, and cousin of Han Liu, Chen Liu's son, who is one of China's assistant vice ministers of foreign affairs.

I read it twice just to be sure I was seeing it correctly. Could this be real? Could this Han Liu be the same person Ashley had written down as Joy's father? The son of China's US ambassador? And a very powerful man in his own right? I couldn't believe it, so I just kept on researching to try to somehow make sense of it. I typed in *Han Liu* and *China assistant vice minister of foreign affairs*. The first photo that popped up stunned me. Han Liu was the same guy from the five-by-seven photograph with Ashley. How was that possible? I kept reading and was again surprised by what I found next. Han Liu had died around four years ago in China. He'd been shot and killed in his home by criminals. Liu was twenty-seven years old. No wife or kids. Two men had been arrested and then publicly executed for Liu's death. I went back further and read a little more background about how Han Liu had been a rising star inside China's government. Many predicted he would one day hold the same office as his father, who was still currently the Chinese ambassador to the United States.

I took a deep breath and let it out slowly. Han Liu had died nearly four years ago. Joy was born three years and two months ago. I looked at the exact date of Liu's death and did quick math in my head. If Liu was somehow her father, he would have died when Ashley was around six weeks pregnant. But how could Ashley have even known the guy? Could she have possibly met him when he was traveling with his father to the US? It would have had to have been a one-night affair or something like that. And I couldn't imagine the woman I married doing the hookup thing with some stranger—especially one who worked for communist China. Plus, they didn't look like a couple who had just met each other in the photograph.

My eyes went back to my phone. I continued to scroll and search, trying to put together whatever pieces I could find. And then my eyes froze on another photo that suddenly showed up on my phone's screen.

I cursed. Agent Chang. The photo was attached to an online news article about Chen Liu, the US ambassador from China. Chen Liu was standing outside a building in Washington, DC, surrounded by reporters. But he was also surrounded by his own security detail. I pinched my fingers on my phone's screen and then spread them to zoom in on the photo. I was certain it was Chang standing directly behind Chen Liu with an earpiece in his right ear.

What did this mean? Was Chang pursuing Ashley on behalf of the Chinese government? If so, why? Because of Joy? Or something else? I again could not fathom how Ashley could've gotten involved with Han Liu. It felt so far out there. She was a secluded painter. I thought back to the first time Ashley had told me about Joy's father.

It was our third official date. A picnic in Ford Park, followed by a concert in the Ford Amphitheater. We'd brought Joy along with us. She was busy going up and down the small slide while Ashley and I sat in two swings next to each other and gently rocked back and forth.

"She's loving this," Ashley said, smiling. "Thanks for including her."

"Of course. I want to spend more time with her. I know she's the most important thing in your life."

"She is. We've been through a lot together in a short amount of time."

"Can't be easy being a single mom."

"No, but she makes it worth it."

"If you don't mind me asking, what happened to her father?"

Ashley had briefly mentioned to me on our first date that Joy's father had died before she was ever born. But I didn't know much else. Ashley hadn't seemed to really want to talk about it thus far.

"Car wreck," she said.

"I'm sorry."

"We were never together. What happened between us was a mistake. But God can redeem a mistake."

Joy was calling out to us to watch her go down the slide for probably the twentieth time. Every time she slid, her face burst with delight.

"Who was he?" I asked.

Ashley shifted a bit in her swing, took a moment to answer. "He owned an art gallery in Laguna Beach."

"Does Joy know much about him?"

"No. I don't have much to tell her. I didn't know him very well myself."

"Did he have family? Do they know about Joy?"

"They were mostly back in China. I never told anyone I was pregnant when I was there, and I left town right after he died."

"Why did you leave?"

She looked over at me with a playful scowl. "You and all your questions."

I laughed. "Sorry. I just want to know the woman who has already captured my heart."

She gave me a coy smile but didn't respond. Then I noticed her face sag, like a sadness had suddenly come over her.

"Hey, what's wrong?" I asked her.

She quickly stood from the swing. "Nothing. We should probably walk over to the concert now so we can grab good seats."

I wondered if Ashley had chosen Kai Lin as Joy's fake father because it was rooted in some actual truth. It wasn't a complete fabrication that would be hard for her to hold together later, when Joy wanted to know more. It would be something she could offer her daughter without having to go down any further roads with it. Kai Lin had little known family. And by all accounts, he'd been a good man who was well thought of in his own community. It was a solid cover. But then I thought about the sadness in her face that day. Was it because of the lies she was already telling me? Or was it something else?

TWENTY-EIGHT

An hour later, I was back on the plane and traveling to Hudson, New York. I still couldn't grasp how Han Liu could possibly be Joy's father. From all accounts I'd found so far online, the important diplomat mostly worked inside China and not in the United States. I exhaustively searched for any mention of trips to the States for Liu during the necessary time period that would coincide with Ashley getting pregnant. But I could find nothing reported during those months. So how could it have even happened? My mind switched gears. Could Ashley have traveled to China? Was that how they'd met? And was that why she was fluent in Chinese?

I doubted Ashley would've written Liu's name on the fake hospital birth certificate if it wasn't the truth. But why had she done it? Why write his name on the fake document but not submit his name to the hospital for the official file? The obvious answer was because she had wanted to hide the truth from everyone but herself. Maybe she wrote it for her own sentimental reasons. But that wouldn't make sense if what she had with Liu was a quick fling. I again studied the five-by-seven photograph. My eyes kept focusing on the rose bouquet Ashley held in her hand. This photograph kept pushing me toward a strange place—one that made even less sense. The photograph did not look like it was one they'd taken on a date. It looked like a wedding photo to me. Was that possible? I didn't want to think about Ashley having possibly been married to another man. And the fact that she would have kept the whole thing secret from me . . . That felt too critical to not share with your future husband.

Still, the thought kept lingering.

Ashley had told me the truth about one thing: Joy's father was indeed dead. But it was nothing like she'd suggested. I thought about Han Liu being shot and killed in China. Was it really at the hands of criminals? Or could it have possibly been about something else? China was known to hide legitimate information—especially when connected to their own government. Which led me back to Kai Lin. Could he have possibly been killed because of his connection to his cousin?

So many questions. So much confusion. My head hurt.

I had to believe the truth behind all this was extremely dangerous, or else Ashley wouldn't be gone right now. She wouldn't have run and not given me the chance to protect her. I stared out the plane window. The sun was going down. Hudson was eight hundred miles from Gatlinburg and just a couple of hours north of New York City. Ashley had had two-month-old Joy with her on the car ride she'd taken from Gatlinburg three years ago—assuming she'd gone straight from Tennessee to New York. That must've been a difficult road trip. What had made her leave Gatlinburg so quickly? Was it Chang? Had he somehow found her there, just like he had in Sedona? Had she been running from Chang this whole time?

We flew into Albany International Airport, which was a forty-five-minute drive to Hudson. It was dark outside by the time we landed. I'd be switching pilots here since they were on airtime restrictions. I again rented a car and was sitting behind the wheel of a Toyota Corolla about twenty minutes after touchdown. Just like I'd found with Gatlinburg, Hudson was a charming little town, located along the banks of the Hudson River. I drove down Warren Street, taking in the shops, boutiques, antique stores, and cafés. The street was still very busy with foot traffic. The last census said Hudson had around six thousand people. It felt clear to me now that Ashley had done her homework and had intentionally chosen each of her moves to put herself in these quaint little art towns. If she was hiding, it probably felt safer to be remote and live outside the big cities. And these places offered her a chance to work on her art and maybe scrounge together a living for her and Joy.

I found myself parked outside a two-story redbrick house with a detached two-story garage a few minutes later. It was the address listed on Ashley's fake driver's license. Laura Hollings. Her hair was still short, but she was now a redhead. She looked so strange to me this way. How exhausting had it been for her to reinvent herself so many times? To change her hair length and color. Had Ashley made up a completely different background story with each move? How had she kept up with it all?

I got out of my rental car, stared at the house. There were lights on outside and in the front windows. The house was small and narrow. Probably only a couple of bedrooms. I glanced over at the garage. It looked to possibly have an apartment above it; I wondered if Ashley had rented that. I walked down a paver front path, stepped up onto a small porch, and glanced inside through a window by the front door. I could see a silver-haired woman walking back and forth across a hallway. I didn't spot anyone else inside the home with her. I knocked on the door and waited. A moment later, the front door opened, and the same woman stood in front of me, wearing a cooking apron over a yellow dress. She was probably in her eighties and had a lively sparkle in her eyes.

"Good evening," I said. "Sorry to bother you, ma'am."

"Oh, it's Birdie. Stop with the 'ma'am' nonsense."

I smiled. "Good to meet you, Birdie. My name is Luke."

"Hi, Luke. What can I do for you?"

I caught a whiff of something pleasant. "It sure does smell great."

"I'm just making some cherry pies. Would you like a slice?"

What a friendly lady. Hopefully, this would work in my favor.

"Maybe." I held up Ashley's fake ID for Laura Hollings. "I was wondering if you remember this woman?"

Birdie took the glasses that were hanging from a thin chain around her neck, slipped them on, and then examined the ID.

"Oh my, yes. I have been praying for her ever since she left."

"Did she live here with you?"

"Yes, next door. Above my garage. With her precious little baby. Are you related to her? Is she doing well?"

I told her the same sad story I'd been using everywhere else, about being her brother and how she was missing.

"That just breaks my heart," she said, putting her hand to her mouth. "She lived with me for about six months. She would help me with work in the garden and around the house. She would often join me for dinner because I love to cook so much. Lexi was such a sweet baby. She would giggle and giggle when I waved my wooden stir spoon around in front of her. I absolutely loved having them here. It was so shocking to me when I knocked on her door one day and she was just gone. All her things cleared out. No word to me at all about leaving."

Ashley had gone through at least three different names for her daughter: Janny, Lexi, and Joy. I couldn't imagine how hard that had been for her. Probably more gut-wrenching than even changing her own name.

"When did she leave?" I asked.

"January fourth, two and a half years ago. I remember very clearly because it was the same day as my sixtieth wedding anniversary to my late husband, George. He's been gone fifteen years, but I still celebrate it. Laura and I had even planned to have tea together that morning to mark the special occasion. But we never got the chance."

I held my phone up to show her a photo of Chang. "Did you ever see this man come around when she was here?"

She leaned in, squinted. "I can't say for sure. I don't think so."

"Did Laura have a job?"

"She worked some over in Patty's flower shop. But it was only part-time because of Lexi. She painted a lot in the garage apartment. She left several of her paintings behind. Do you want to see them?"

"Yes, please."

"Follow me."

I trailed Birdie over to the two-bay garage unit. She opened a side door and flicked on a light. There was a white Buick in the first slot; the other spot was empty. The walls of the garage were lined with tall metal shelves and stocked full of various dusty boxes and plastic tubs. Birdie must've lived here for a long time. She scooted around the front of the Buick and over to the far wall. She had a gray sheet over the paintings. When she pulled it off, dust exploded into the air. It didn't seem to bother the elderly woman.

"Here they are," she said. "Just beautiful."

I walked over and began flipping through six different canvases. They were Ashley's; I recognized the same beautiful landscapes she'd become known for in Vail. Rivers, mountains, and gardens. Some of the paintings were half-finished. Picking one up to hold in better light, I found my fingers touching something on the backside of the canvas. It was a white envelope stuck up in the corner behind the frame. I pulled it out.

"She also left that behind," Birdie mentioned. "So I stuck it in with the paintings in case she ever came back."

Opening the envelope, I found a couple of glossy four-by-six photographs inside. They were all group photos, Ashley standing with several other young guys and gals her age. She looked college-age. Maybe twenty. Her hair was long and light brown, just like it was in the photograph with Han Liu. She wore jeans and a gray sweatshirt. They were standing outside in front of a brick building. One of the photos had them surrounding a man whom I thought I recognized. A politician?

He was probably fiftysomething, and wearing a gray suit. They were all posing for the camera and smiling wide. I noticed that four from the group all had on the same brown T-shirt. My eyes narrowed on what was printed on the front of the shirts: Go Forth International Missions.

My eyes narrowed. International Missions?

Could that be how Ashley had gotten to China?

TWENTY-NINE

I held on to the envelope of photos, quickly downed a slice of cherry pie, thanked Birdie, and then left in a hurry. I was eager to look further into Go Forth International Missions. Was Ashley part of this group? Was that why she'd been photographed standing with others wearing the same T-shirt? Just around the corner from Birdie's house, I pulled off and stopped in an empty parking lot outside a tiny post office building. Sitting in my rental car, I began a Google search on my phone for the mission organization. It was not difficult to find information about them. The entire first page of my search was loaded with news articles and stories. But nearly all of them had been published around the same time six years ago. And they were all about the exact same thing—which shook me to my core. I began scanning the headlines, each one feeling like a punch to the gut that knocked the wind out of me.

"Sarah Bowman, 20, Missionary, Dead in China"

"Arrested Missionary Girl Dies in China Jail"

"Missions Group Shocked Over Death of College Girl"

"Missionary Dead, China Denies Foul Play"

There were dozens more just like these listed all down the page. I clicked on the first article, from the *Richmond Times-Dispatch*, and immediately stared at a photo of my wife at twenty. Ashley looked like she had in the group photographs I'd just found at Birdie's house. The article said that twenty-year-old Sarah Bowman of Middleburg, Virginia, had died in a Chinese jail two days after being arrested for street evangelism, which is illegal in China. Sarah was part of a college missionary group from Go Forth International Missions and traveling in China for a month. No one else from the group of ten had been arrested or harmed. The mission organization was urgently coordinating efforts to bring the rest of the group home to the United States as soon as possible. China denied any involvement in Bowman's unexpected death. United States officials were working to recover her body.

I sat there, stunned. Ashley was Sarah Bowman.

I clicked on the next story, from the *Virginia-Pilot*. It was basically the same information but had a quote from the head of Go Forth International Missions: "We are shocked and horrified about what has happened to Sarah Bowman. We've been told by those on-site that Sarah boldly put herself in jeopardy, despite warnings by local police authorities, to spread the gospel to a group of children. We are desperately trying to get more answers. Our prayers are with Sarah's mother."

Her mother? Ashley didn't have a mother. I shook my head, recognizing it was stupid to assume I knew anything anymore. So much of what I'd thought I knew were lies. I continued clicking on more articles, looking for further details, each an out-of-body experience. I finally found an article that included a quote from Sarah Bowman's mother, Janny Bowman. "Sarah was a ray of sunlight in a dark world. Despite a difficult childhood, she brought life into every room she entered. Her heart was her best attribute. A heart for God and for others. She wanted to make a difference in this world. I'm so heartbroken."

Now I knew who the Janny was from the handwritten note I'd found in Ashley's hidden black bag: her mother. Janny Bowman's name popped up in several more articles about Sarah's death, with additional quotes, all basically saying the same thing: how heartbroken she was about her daughter's death. One of the articles mentioned that Janny had adopted Sarah out of foster care when she was fourteen years old. So Ashley had not entirely been lying about her childhood experience. She'd just omitted the final few teenage years. I needed to track down Janny Bowman. This thought was immediately dashed after I scrolled farther down the page and found a brief obituary four years ago from an outlet called *Middleburg Life*. Janny Bowman. She'd lived in Middleburg for fifty-eight years after her family moved to Virginia from Alabama when she was seven years old. She was preceded in death by her husband, Carl, and her daughter, Sarah, and survived by her younger sister, Claudia Bishop, also of Middleburg.

So Ashley's mother was unfortunately dead. I took a deep breath, sat back in my seat, tried to somehow process all this shocking new information. Ashley had gone on a mission trip in college. She'd been arrested and proclaimed dead. Only she clearly wasn't dead. She was very much alive. So what had happened? Much of my trail about Ashley's life before me began in Laguna Beach four years ago. That was two years after she had been reported dead in China. What had happened in between? Where was she, and what had she been doing for more than two years? I felt like I knew one thing for sure: whatever it was, she was currently on the run from it.

I looked back at the article mentioning Janny Bowman's sister, Claudia Bishop, who would've been Ashley's aunt. Was she still around? I did another search and, after some scrolling, found a Facebook profile for Claudia Bishop of Middleburg, Virginia. I clicked on it. Claudia had short gray-brown hair and looked to be in her early sixties. Her Facebook page showed a recent posting. Claudia was huddled around a table with some friends at a restaurant called King Street Oyster Bar. Her post said: Celebrating ten years with the crazy gals of our book club! Another search showed King Street Oyster Bar to be at 1 East

Washington Street, Middleburg, Virginia. It appeared that Claudia was still alive and well in Middleburg. I wondered if she would be able to tell me more about Ashley, her life, and what had happened in the aftermath of her reported death. I needed to talk to someone in the know. And it looked like Go Forth International Missions had shut down operations within the same year as Sarah Bowman's death.

After not being able to locate any type of phone number online for Claudia Bishop, I decided to send her a direct message through Facebook. Hopefully, she was active on social media and would respond promptly.

> Hi Claudia, I hope this finds you doing well. My name is Luke Driskell. I would very much like to talk to you about your late niece, Sarah Bowman. I don't know exactly how to say this, but she was very special to me. Please call me or respond to this message as soon as possible. Thank you.

I included my phone number. I wasn't exactly sure what I would say to Claudia to explain why her niece had been special to me. But I felt like I needed to add that line so she wouldn't think I was a reporter or something. Or else I might not get a response.

I started scrolling some more, continuing to read articles from the week that Sarah Bowman had died in China. Some follow-up stories said China was not cooperating in returning her body to the United States. I shook my head. Of course not. Because there was no body. I found one article that gave me more background information about my wife. She'd been a sophomore at the University of Virginia, where she'd studied education, and had wanted to eventually be a teacher. Before that, she'd attended John Champe High School in Aldie, Virginia, where she played volleyball, sang in the choir, and was part of the art club. It was a surreal feeling to be finding out the truth about my wife's childhood from news articles that were all tied to reporting about her tragic death.

I took another deep breath, let it out slowly, tried to decide what to do next. I obviously wasn't staying in Hudson, New York. And I wasn't going back to Vail right now. I looked down at my phone again.

Ashley was from Middleburg, Virginia.

I needed to go there.

THIRTY

I booked a hotel room at the St. Regis in Washington, DC, and then drove back to the Albany airport. Since I would be arriving late, I planned to stay the night in DC and head over to Middleburg tomorrow morning. Ashley's hometown was not too far across the state border. Surely I would get a reply or phone call from Claudia Bishop between now and then. It was a quick hour-long flight down to Reagan International. I spent the entire time with my face planted in my phone, searching nonstop for as much information about Sarah Bowman as I could find.

There were local newspaper mentions of her exploits with her high school volleyball team, who had made it to the state playoffs her junior year. She was part of a church youth group that put on special events for assisted-living centers. She'd won several local art contests. I even found an old social media account that belonged to her that had never been deleted. She'd posted pictures with her friends, goofing off and having fun. Just normal teenagers. By all accounts, she'd had an enjoyable high school experience. Which was not at all what she'd told me. I stared out the plane's window into the dark sky. This made me think about a conversation we'd had early on in our courtship.

It made so much more sense now.

We were having dinner at a window table at Matsuhisa, a fabulous Japanese restaurant with views straight up Vail Mountain. It was snowing hard outside, which made for a pretty scene. Ski season was swiftly approaching, and I looked forward to taking Ashley up on the mountain because she still had not tried skiing since moving to Eagle. She was reluctant, but I promised to guide her each step of the way. I wanted to spend every moment possible with her—even buried in the powder on the mountain.

"Beautiful," Ashley said, staring out the window at the falling snow.

"Indeed," I replied.

But I wasn't staring out the window; I was looking directly at her. She noticed this and gave me a shy smile. "Have you always been this forward with girls?"

"Never. Just you. I can't help myself."

"I bet you always say that, too."

I laughed. "No, it's true. I was always reserved as a kid. In high school, I could hardly ever find the courage to ask out girls, even though I knew a lot of them liked me because I was on the basketball team. I don't know what it was. I think I was just so ashamed of my poor living situation that I didn't want any of the girls to see it up close. I wanted to hide it."

"It couldn't have been that bad."

"Believe me, it was. When I sold my grandfather's property after leaving for college, the new owners didn't even want the trailer. I think they had it hauled off to the junkyard. What about you? The guys must've been chasing after you in high school. Did you date a lot?"

"Hardly."

"Why? I'm sure you were a looker even then."

"No one wants to date the foster kid, believe me. It isn't cool."

"I think it's damn cool."

She smiled, picked at her sushi. Apparently, she didn't want to expound on the topic. But I pressed forward anyway.

"When was the last time you were back in your hometown?"

"The day I left for college."

"For real?"

"Why would I want to return to the source of so much pain?"

"I don't know. Closure? It was good for me to go back to Seguin several years ago after I became a success. Put things into perspective. Helped me to appreciate the hard stuff I went through to get to where I am today. I bolted town so fast back then that I never really said goodbye."

"Well, I said goodbye the day I left. And I'm never going back."

"Never?"

"Never."

I thought about that now. Ashley couldn't go back. But the roadblock was something much more significant than her hometown being a source of her pain. Everyone there believed she was dead. And she clearly wanted to preserve that. Before her mission trip, Ashley seemed to have been a normal, fun-loving college girl, with all her hopes and dreams ahead of her—and then everything had dramatically changed in China.

I still didn't know how or why.

THIRTY-ONE

Upon landing in DC, I checked my voice mails while walking through Reagan International on the way to pick up my rental car. The third one I listened to—from an unidentified number—stopped me in my tracks. *"Mr. Driskell, this is Special Agent Evan McGregor with the Federal Bureau of Investigation. I need you to call me back immediately, sir, no matter the time of day. This is a very urgent situation. Your prompt response is critical to one of our investigations. You must call us back."* The time stamp said it had been left forty-two minutes ago. I noticed a voice mail further down from the same number, left ten minutes ago. I pressed Play. *"This is Special Agent McGregor calling again. I need to hear from you, Mr. Driskell. It is very important. Call me ASAP."*

I had not been answering any phone calls today. There was little doubt in my mind they'd finally discovered Danny Lamar. And clearly, by looking into his work, they'd found out about his involvement with me. I now knew I was working against the clock. I had only so long to not respond to them before it got me into more serious trouble. From the tone in the FBI agent's voice, I knew they would not sit around waiting for my phone call for very long. They would come looking for me. And I wouldn't be too hard to find. Unlike Ashley, I had no fake IDs; I was traveling as myself. That would be easy for the FBI to track.

I drove into DC proper and valeted my rental car at the St. Regis. I'd stayed there a few times before on business travel. The hotel sat a couple of blocks north of the White House. After checking into my room around midnight, I tossed my travel bag on the bed. I was ready to also toss myself onto the bed. I felt completely exhausted. I hadn't slept much at all in several days. But I was starving. I had made little time to eat anything properly while flying around the country. I searched my phone for late-night food options and found the Old Ebbitt Grill was open until two in the morning. It was only a five-minute walk from the hotel.

I left my room—hungrier than ever—took the elevator down, and found the sidewalk outside the hotel. After walking around the vast White House property, I located the tavern-style restaurant a block over. It was still surprisingly busy. I made my way to the bar, grabbed a stool, and snagged a menu lying on the bar top next to me. I immediately wanted to order half of what was in it. I started with some chicken wings and a glass of bourbon. Sitting there, I started going through more of my voice mails. Everyone seemed to be looking for me: the Vail police detective, Doug Pederson at the TV station, Mark and Susan, other friends, and even my business partners. I had intentionally gone completely off the map. It felt so bizarre to be sitting here in this iconic DC saloon after midnight, with all this new information I'd discovered about Ashley. Who else knew the truth about her? Anyone other than perhaps a former CIA agent and Chinese security officials?

For probably the thousandth time, I pulled up the Find My app on my phone to see if I could locate Ashley's GPS signal. I wasn't sure I'd ever stop trying. But there was no signal. I looked at the time on my phone. 12:32 a.m. I did quick math. It had been nearly seventy-three hours since the last time I spoke with Ashley. In some ways, it felt like I'd just had that phone conversation with her in the hospital. In other ways, it felt like months had already passed, because so much had happened in between. Would I ever see her again? I'd been fiercely fighting to believe it. But with each passing hour, I felt my grip on hope weakening.

I finished my bourbon, requested another round. After devouring my chicken wings, I ordered the Chesapeake Bay blue catfish sandwich, which I ate within five minutes of its arrival. It felt good to squash my hunger pangs. After paying, I began my trek back to my hotel. I was walking up 15th Street NW when I spotted something behind me out of the corner of my eye: a black Escalade with tinted windows. I noticed it because it was driving very slowly while other cars and taxis zipped around it. I stopped for a moment, bent down like I was tying my shoe, peered back again. The Escalade pulled up to the curb.

Was someone following me?

Standing, I started to walk again and took a quick glance. The Escalade was back on the road and creeping forward. I made a left at the next cross street, H Street NW, and then really picked up my pace. I tossed another peek over my shoulder, cursed. The Escalade had also turned on H Street NW. What the hell? Who could be following me? Who would even know I was in DC right now? Could the FBI have already tracked me down? I doubted it, or else they would have already stopped me. It was unnerving to have someone trailing me. Were they waiting to see where I went? If they knew I was at the restaurant, they'd probably followed me from the St. Regis. Were they waiting to grab me somewhere?

This sent a charge through me. I was approaching Lafayette Square, which was several historic acres of public park a block north of the White House. My stress level building, I decided to use the park to make a run for it. I doubted whoever was driving the Escalade would jump the curb and drive through a park that sat only a few hundred feet from the White House.

I bolted forward into the grassy area, circled around the enormous Andrew Jackson statue in the middle, before taking my first look back. I cursed again. Two men were now out of the Escalade and pursuing me. It was too dark to tell what they looked like. I also wasn't staying around long enough to find out. I raced forward again, my long legs hammering through the grass, running as fast as I possibly could. I made it through the park and onto Pennsylvania Avenue on the other side. But I didn't slow down. I continued to sprint up the sidewalk, away from the park, hoping my dash for freedom wasn't somehow interpreted by any nearby Secret Service as a threat to the White House. I made it three full blocks before I finally tucked myself away in an alley between buildings. I moved deep into it and then slid down behind a metal dumpster. For a second, I wondered if I'd made a foolish mistake. I couldn't see an exit out the other side of the alley. If the two guys followed me in, I was a sitting duck.

Peering around the dumpster, I watched the street closely. Five minutes passed without any sign of my pursuers. Then ten minutes. I was starting to catch my breath. Surely I had lost them. I waited a full twenty minutes before I found the courage to make my way back to the sidewalk. I studied all sides of the street around me. I didn't see the guys anywhere. I also didn't spot the black Escalade. I took a deep breath, let it out slowly. I wasn't sure what to do next. It probably wasn't wise to go back to the St. Regis. They might be waiting for me there. I couldn't even chance going back for my travel bag or my rental car. I needed to switch hotels. I probably also needed to pay for it in cash. I had no clue what I was up against right now. They could be tracking me through my credit card usage. My only option was likely cheap motels since most nicer hotels asked for credit cards.

I needed to buy myself time—at least another day. I stared at my phone, wondered if they could be tracking me through it. It was certainly possible. But tossing it meant eliminating any possibility of hearing from Ashley again. I couldn't fathom doing that. I would have to risk the phone. I found the closest ATM and used my debit card to withdraw $500, the maximum amount. Then I began a long walk to find safe lodging for the rest of the night.

THIRTY-TWO

I slept horribly on an uncomfortable bed in a Motel 6 near the convention center and was up well before sunrise because of it. My back ached, and I had a crick in my neck. Apparently, Claudia Bishop was also an early riser, because I got a Facebook message from her while splashing water on my face in the tiny bathroom. I grabbed my phone. The battery was running low. I would need to pick up a portable charger that morning to keep it from dying, since I'd left my other charging cords in my travel bag.

Claudia: Hi Luke, I'd be happy to speak with you about our precious Sarah. I still miss her tremendously. Do you want to talk on the phone today?

I immediately replied, hoping to catch her still online: Can we meet this morning? I'm close to Middleburg.

She got right back to me. Of course. How about the Common Grounds off West Washington at 9am? Their breakfast sandwiches are delicious.

I replied: Perfect! Thank you. See you at 9.

I set my phone down, feeling relieved. While I'd been prepared to drive out to Middleburg even if I hadn't heard from Claudia, I was grateful to not have to waste time tracking her down once I got there.

I put on the same clothes I'd worn the day before because I had nothing else, then tried to straighten my hair in the mirror using only wet fingers. It was a bit of a mess. I needed hair cream and other toiletries. I couldn't even brush my teeth. But all that was certainly not a priority at the moment.

Getting ready to head out the door, I picked up my phone again, stared down at my voice mails. I'd received two more urgent messages from Special Agent Evan McGregor. One had come in at two in the morning—he obviously didn't care if he woke me—and then one had arrived just thirty minutes ago. With each call, I could tell the special agent was getting more and more agitated about my lack of response. But he had not yet threatened to hunt me down. I figured that was probably coming soon.

I left my motel room and walked to the sidewalk on the street. The sun was now starting to rise over the city, and morning traffic was picking up steam. It took me a few minutes to wave down a taxi. At this point, I wanted to travel using only my cash. No credit cards.

"You mind driving out to Middleburg?" I asked the driver, a chubby guy named Jed in a black fedora. It was about an hour away.

"Sure, if you tip big. Gotta drive all the way back, ya know."

I handed him a hundred dollars. "Tip in advance."

"Cool, let's go."

We drove past the US Capitol Building and then eventually across the Arland Williams Memorial Bridge into Virginia. I couldn't stop thinking about the two guys from the black Escalade. The image of them pursuing me through Lafayette Square had bounced around in my head all night long. Had they just been trying to trail me? Or had they been attempting to grab me and haul me away somewhere? I feared the latter. Who were they? CIA? Chinese security? Someone else? I didn't want to have to deal with any of these possibilities. But I couldn't shake the thought that they may have been tracking me across the country yesterday.

My driver wasn't much of a chatterbox, which was good since I mostly wanted to be on my phone. I couldn't stop reading all the articles about Sarah Bowman's tragic death in China six years ago. It was so difficult to imagine Ashley being thrown into a foreign jail and then whatever came next. She was only twenty years old. She had to have been scared out of her mind. I had so many questions flooding my brain. Had they hurt her? Had they tortured her? How had she finally gotten away? How had she made her way back to the United States? Would I ever get the truth? Would I ever see my wife and stepdaughter again? Every place I'd visited yesterday had the exact same theme: Ashley had bolted town nearly overnight. And they never heard from her again. Would that also be my story? I'd survived a lot in my life. But I wasn't sure I'd survive losing Ashley and Joy.

I stared out the car window, tried not to think too much about it. We finally arrived in Middleburg. Common Grounds was off the main street in the center of the small town. My taxi driver pulled over to the curb.

I leaned forward. "How much to hang around in case I'm only here for a brief time?"

"Make it worth my while."

I handed him nearly all my cash. "This keep you here and get me back to DC?"

He quickly skimmed it. "That should do the trick."

"Great. Why don't you just park around the corner?"

"Will do."

I got out of the taxi. I was early. I still had thirty minutes before I was supposed to meet with Claudia Bishop. I'd noticed a Safeway grocery store just up the street and began walking in that direction. Once inside, I found the ATM and pulled out another five hundred in cash. If anyone was tracking my debit card transactions, they could find me here. But how fast could they get to Middleburg? Hopefully, I had enough time to have this conversation and still get out of town. It felt surreal to even be having this train of thought running through my head. What had happened to my life? I did some quick shopping inside Safeway. I found a black backpack in the school-supply section. Then I grabbed the necessary toiletries: toothpaste, toothbrush, hair cream, deodorant, soap, and shampoo. Finally, I found charging cords for my phone, along with a portable charger. I paid for the items at the front and then walked back over to Common Grounds.

Stepping inside, I did a quick scan of the place. It was a cool little coffeehouse with a warm feel. Although the place was half-full, I didn't see anyone who resembled Claudia Bishop. I found a table in the corner by the window. After sitting, I opened the portable charger I'd just purchased and plugged it into my phone. Thankfully, it was precharged and began rescuing my phone from the dreaded red bar. Staring out the window, I wondered how many times Ashley had been inside this same coffeehouse. She must've walked up and down this street a thousand times. She had said she'd never return to this place. And now I was sitting here. Surreal. Even under the dire circumstances, I felt a deep connection to her. I wanted to go into every store and ask about Sarah Bowman. I wanted to know people who knew her.

But first, Claudia Bishop, whom I spotted walking up the sidewalk and entering the door a few seconds later.

I stood, approached her. "Claudia?"

"Luke?"

"Yes, ma'am. Thank you so much for coming. Can I buy you breakfast?"

She smiled. "Coffee would be great."

We stepped up to the counter together and both ordered coffee. Then we made our way over to my table with our cups and sat opposite of each other.

Claudia said, "I noticed on your Facebook page you live in Colorado."

"Yes, I live in Vail."

"I've never been to Colorado, but I hear it is beautiful."

"I enjoy it very much."

I had figured she would probably look at my page when she got my direct message. I hadn't posted anything since I met Ashley—especially because she never wanted her photo on social media. So I wasn't concerned that Claudia would see anything that would blow my cover.

"So how did you know Sarah?" she asked me.

"Sarah and I had corresponded online quite a bit when she was at UVA. I was a graduate student studying art history. We had an online class together. I really enjoyed getting to know her, even though we never met in person. For some reason, I'd been thinking about her a lot lately and felt compelled to come here while traveling to DC."

I'd come up with this lie during the night while staring at the ceiling with a broken spring in my back. I obviously couldn't tell her the truth, even though she was the first family member with whom I'd ever spoken. Claudia seemed to easily accept this story.

"Sarah was something special," she said. "I still cry when I think too much about what happened to her."

"It must've been devastating. I didn't know her well, but it still really hit me hard, even from across the country. I couldn't believe it."

"None of us could. The whole town was in shock for a while. It crushed my sister, Sarah's mother. Sadly, she never really recovered."

"Did you ever get more details about what happened to Sarah?"

"Nothing. The mission organization tried their best to get answers but never really got anywhere. Chinese officials claimed Sarah simply died in her sleep the second night in jail. Of course, we could never verify any of that. Getting information from the Chinese was next to impossible. I think some of our own government officials tried to help but never really got anywhere, either. Then it all just kind of faded away, despite my sister's relentless pleading."

"What did your sister do?"

Claudia sighed. "Janny must've written two dozen emails to Senator Pullson, begging him for help to at least get Sarah's body back. He replied to her first two emails, telling her they were doing everything they could. But then he stopped replying altogether."

It clicked that Senator Pullson of Virginia was the politician I'd recognized in the group photo.

"I saw a photo of Senator Pullson with the mission group."

She nodded. "He actually came to the send-off when they were leaving. I think he was somehow connected with the head of the organization. He even said a nice prayer and all. That's why Janny kept writing him."

"But Sarah's body was never returned?"

"Sadly, no. And there was nothing we could do about it. I think without that closure, my sister just cracked. She would just sit in her rocking chair in the corner of her living room and stare blankly at the walls all day. I could hardly get her to eat anything. She just lost all motivation to live. At the very end, she lost her mind entirely."

"What happened?" I asked.

"She claimed she got a phone call from Sarah, if you can believe it."

That made me sit up straight. "What?"

Claudia sighed, shook her head. "Yeah, she told me she got a call out of nowhere. Sarah was alive and was coming to see her."

"You think she'd just become delusional?"

"Yes. She'd lost touch with reality. Because she was adamant that she was telling me the truth. She even sent another email to Senator Pullson to tell him about the phone call and ask him to look into the situation again."

I pitched my head. "Did he respond to her?"

"I don't know. She died the next day."

"How?"

"She drowned in her bathtub."

"That's awful, Claudia. I'm so sorry."

"The odd thing was that Janny rarely took baths. So I often wondered if it was suicide. That maybe my sister was in so much emotional pain that she went under the water and never came back up again."

"How long ago did Janny die?" I asked.

Claudia thought about it a moment. "It was four years ago last month. But it still feels like it happened yesterday. I miss her so much."

Four years ago was when Ashley had made a reappearance as Amy Sundown in Laguna Beach. The phone call to Janny had likely been real. But someone must've been watching and listening. Was it the Chinese? I thought about Senator Pullson, whom Janny had emailed right before she drowned in the bathtub. Could he have possibly been involved? Had Ashley's mother been murdered? Had someone staged it to look like a drowning? Was this whole thing much bigger than I even thought?

THIRTY-THREE

I was back in the taxi again and heading to DC. Ashley had reached out to Janny, her mother, upon returning to the United States four years ago. Could it be a coincidence that her mother drowned in the bathtub two days later? Especially when Claudia had claimed her sister rarely even took baths? I doubted it. It must've been devastating for Ashley when she found out what happened to her mother. My wife had been through more than I could've ever imagined—and I still didn't know the full extent of it.

I again thought about Kai Lin in Laguna Beach. His partner at the art gallery had told me Kai was helping Ashley with a "situation." It had to have been connected to all this. And then Kai Lin had wound up dead. That was two people Ashley had reached out to for help who'd both ended up dead—one shot in the back and dumped into the bay, the other drowned in her own bathtub. I now knew why Ashley likely had never pulled me into the truth. She'd been protecting me. But now I desperately wanted to protect her.

Which meant I couldn't stop searching for answers—even if it was putting my own life on the line. And the only person I knew to speak with next was a powerful DC politician. I did some quick research on Senator Ted Pullson in the back of the taxi. He'd grown up in Leesburg,

Virginia, which was only eighteen miles up the road from Middleburg. He had quickly worked his way up the governmental ranks with various important jobs before eventually becoming head of the CIA for seven years. He'd then run for office. At sixty years old, Pullson had held his senate seat since 2012. He was currently on the United States Senate Select Committee on Intelligence and the Subcommittee on Terrorism, Technology and Homeland Security. I kept digging and digging. I quickly became aware of how intricately involved Pullson was with China affairs. There had been lots of articles written about it over the years.

I did another quick search, grouping Senator Pullson with Go Forth International Missions. I found one hit, a press release from the mission group from six years ago. It included the same group photo of the ten college students standing with Senator Pullson, along with a quote: "I commend these ten young men and women for their courage to go into places that are resistant to Christianity in order to share their faith. I have been to China many times. I have personally seen what a dark place it is spiritually. Please join me in praying that their journey will be safe and will yield meaningful results."

How would I find Pullson? Was he even in DC right now? I looked up the senate calendar and found they were currently in session, so he was likely around. I went to Pullson's political website, but there was no schedule or calendar listed for him—not that I expected to find one. I was just searching for anything I could think of to try to come up with a way to talk to him. Pullson had official accounts on every social media platform. But they were likely run by interns and only showcased him at various events. I went to Twitter and did a search within the app for *Senator Pullson*. I then went to the "Latest" posts that had tagged his official account. This was when I found something useful—a new DC Italian restaurant called Carmelo's was having their official grand opening at lunchtime today. The post showed a photo of the front of a restaurant with a message that read: We are excited to have @tedpullson join us for our ribbon cutting today at noon. Senator Pullson and Carmelo have been long time friends. Please come out.

It was ten forty. I would be back in DC in plenty of time. But how would I even talk to the guy? What kind of security would be around a sitting senator? How close to him could I even get?

I was about to find out.

THIRTY-FOUR

Carmelo's was only two blocks from the Russell Senate Office Building. I stood on a busy corner across the street and watched what looked like a lot prep work going on by restaurant staff inside and outside the building. There was an outdoor patio with several tables covered in white linen cloths. I could see a fiftysomething guy in a white chef's coat, zipping in and out with a bit of a frantic look on his face. Probably Carmelo himself. He clearly wanted everything perfect for the grand opening, which was to take place in fifteen minutes. I looked down at my phone when it buzzed in my hand. I shook my head. It was Special Agent Evan McGregor again. I had stopped listening to his voice mails. I didn't even want to know what he had to say at this point because it would only further stress me out. I was running out of time. I couldn't avoid his phone calls forever.

Fifteen minutes later, a bigger crowd had gathered on the sidewalk outside the restaurant. It must have included a segment of the media because I could see a camera guy and a young female reporter with a microphone. But no sign of Senator Pullson yet. I hoped there hadn't been a change of plans. Carmelo, the man in the chef's coat, was shaking hands and chatting with the group of people huddled around the outdoor-patio area. Then I noticed a black Suburban pull up to the curb in a spot that had been blocked off with cones near the front of the restaurant. A young guy in a black suit got out first, followed by Senator Pullson, who was also in a suit. It didn't look like there were any security guys with the senator. Carmelo immediately came over and shook hands with Pullson, who smiled and patted him on the back.

Clutching my black backpack over my shoulder, I waited for traffic to clear and then quickly made my way to the other side of the street. I stood near the back of the group of people. A guy with a mandolin began playing upbeat music—a cue the ceremony was about to begin. A man with bright-white hair and wearing a white suit approached a microphone. He introduced himself as Roddy Whitman. He was apparently some kind of local radio host. He then began welcoming everyone and talking about what an awesome guy Carmelo Rossi was and all the success he'd had with other restaurants in town over the years. I mostly watched Pullson, who stood over to the side next to Carmelo and the guy in the black suit, who was probably his aide. I wondered how long Pullson would stay around. Would he say a few nice things and then immediately bolt? Just in case, I shifted my way around the back of the crowd and over toward the parked Suburban.

Roddy Whitman was making everyone laugh with his boisterous personality. Carmelo then spoke, followed by Pullson, who told a funny story about meeting the young chef fifteen years ago after complaining about his meal at another restaurant. When Pullson finished, a lady in a pantsuit pulled out a giant pair of scissors. Two more staff members stretched out a huge red ribbon right in front of the main doors. Pullson took the scissors, and then he and Carmelo and several others posed for a few pictures from several photographers. Finally, Pullson cut the ribbon, everyone clapped, and the mandolin player struck up his music again.

I watched Pullson, to see if he was hanging around or leaving. He shook hands for about ten minutes with a lot of people around and then walked with his aide toward the Suburban. I was standing only a few feet away from the back door they'd stepped out of moments ago. It was time for me to make my move and see what came of it.

"Senator Pullson, could I speak to you for a brief moment?"

He gave me a quick dismissive look. "Sorry, I'm in a hurry."

His aide opened the back door for him.

"It's about Sarah Bowman," I said.

He paused, glanced back at me. "Who?"

"Sarah Bowman, the missing missionary girl from six years ago."

He turned to fully face me. "You mean the dead missionary girl."

"Maybe. Can I have a moment?"

His eyes narrowed. "Who are you?"

"A member of Sarah's family."

He sighed. "Look, I don't really have time for this right now. As I've said many times over the years, I'm really sorry about what happened to Sarah. It was such a tragedy. I know it must continue to be a difficult thing for the family to deal with. None of us will ever get over what happened. But we must try. My prayers continue to be with you and your family."

"Janny Bowman, Sarah's mother, believed Sarah was still alive."

He gave me a sad frown. "I can assure you that's not true."

"How?"

"Listen, I have to go now."

He turned to get into the Suburban.

I pressed. "What about the phone call from Sarah that Janny emailed you about four years ago?"

His head snapped back around, and he glared at me for a full two seconds. "I don't know what you're talking about."

"I have a copy of the email."

I was lying, of course. I just wanted to see his response. His face was getting redder. This made me suspicious. Pullson had to somehow be involved. Otherwise, he wouldn't look this agitated.

"What was your name again?" he asked me.

"It's not important."

He stepped toward me. "You're not really family, are you?"

"Of course I am."

"Then show me some ID."

"I'm just asking for your help, Senator."

"You don't want my help. This is an ambush. You're working with that troublemaker, Jeff Roberts, aren't you? Trying to make something out of nothing again. Let that girl rest in peace already."

"Senator, why could we never recover Sarah's body?" I asked.

"I have to go."

At that point, he climbed into the Suburban, followed by his aide. Seconds later, the vehicle pulled away from the curb. I watched it drive off and then processed our entire exchange. Pullson clearly knew more than he was willing to share; I was convinced of that. I didn't recognize the name Jeff Roberts. Who was he? I needed to find that out next.

THIRTY-FIVE

It was not difficult for me to track down Jeff Roberts. He was an investigative reporter for the *Washington Post*, assuming it was the same one Pullson had just mentioned. Why had Pullson called him a troublemaker? Had Roberts been investigating what had really happened to Ashley? I did exhaustive searching online but couldn't find any articles or stories he'd written about Sarah Bowman's death. Although I couldn't locate a phone number for Roberts, I did find his newspaper email listed.

I typed up a quick message to him.

> Mr. Roberts, I urgently need to speak with you. It's about Sarah Bowman and Senator Pullson. Long story short, I know things I believe you would find interesting. Please call, text, or email ASAP.

I left my phone number, hit Send. Hopefully, Roberts was the kind of guy who incessantly checked his emails. Most reporters I knew did. Their faces were always stuck three inches from their phones.

I then hailed a taxi and headed back to my room at Motel 6. I hadn't checked out, because I wasn't sure what the day would entail.

Plus, I badly needed a shower now that I had my own toiletries. I walked into my first-floor motel room, set my backpack on the bed, and then turned on the shower. While I got undressed, my phone buzzed. I picked it up. An unidentified DC phone number. It had to be Roberts.

"Hello?" I asked.

"You the guy who sent me the email?"

"Yes. Thanks for calling."

"What's this about?"

"You remember the Sarah Bowman story?"

"Sort of. I just refreshed my memory by looking it up. Who are you?"

"A family friend."

"You the guy who went on the news a few days ago who put up a million dollars trying to find his wife?"

"How did you—"

"This isn't amateur hour, Luke. What's your angle here?"

I guess I shouldn't have been surprised he'd researched me before making the phone call. He was an investigative reporter, after all, and he probably wanted to see in advance if I was some kind of whack job. Because I had no other option, I had used my personal email account. I had little doubt the first things listed on Google for me right now were all about my time in front of the TV cameras on *Good Morning, Denver*.

"Yes, but this isn't about that."

"Right. Then why don't you tell me what this is about?"

He clearly didn't believe me. I wanted to tread carefully. "Were you ever investigating a story involving Sarah Bowman and Senator Pullson?"

"Why're you asking?"

"Because Pullson just told me straight to my face you were a troublemaker about it."

"Pullson said that?" He kind of laughed. "It was a nonstory four years ago. I got an email from Sarah Bowman's mother telling me that her daughter was alive. She was asking for my help. She mentioned in her email that she'd also asked Pullson for help. I was on vacation at the time. So I had my phone completely off. When I got back, I responded to the email. She never got back to me. I found out later she had died."

"You ever talk to Pullson about it?"

"Yeah, I did. He denied ever getting an email from her. I probed around a bit, kind of pissed him off, but never really got anywhere. So I dropped it. You got some kind of new angle you want to share with me?"

"Maybe. Can we meet up?"

"Why don't you just tell me on the phone?"

"I'd rather speak with you in person."

I wasn't sure what all I wanted to share with him just yet. I needed serious help, but I didn't think I should reveal everything. I wanted to buy some time to come up with my own version of the truth.

He sighed, irritated. "Yeah, all right. But this better be good. I'm a busy man. Meet me at Capital Burger in an hour. If your info is worthless, you're going to at least buy me lunch."

He hung up. I grabbed my new shampoo and soap and hopped in the shower. The motel at least had hot water. I scrubbed myself up good and soaked for a bit while I tried to figure out what I should and shouldn't tell Roberts. I needed to share enough to somehow motivate him to investigate. He likely had sources inside the government who might be able to tell me something about what really happened with Ashley. But I didn't want this further exposing my wife and potentially putting her in even more danger. It was a slippery slope. I got out of the shower, put on deodorant, brushed my teeth, and then fixed my hair. Finally, I put my dirty clothes back on and headed for the door.

When I opened it, I froze.

THIRTY-SIX

Two men stood right outside the door, both wearing black ski masks and military-green shirts and pants. They immediately charged me, tackling me to the tattered carpet, knocking the breath out of me. I tried to fight back, but they were both much stronger than me. One of them pinned me to the floor while the other put the barrel of a gun to the center of my forehead. I stopped struggling, stayed perfectly still. I'd never been more frightened in my life.

The guy with the gun leaned in close to my face. "Why're you asking questions about a dead girl?"

I wasn't sure what to say. I was too terrified to even speak.

The guy continued, "If you want to stay alive, you'll shut your damn mouth and walk away from this right now. Do you understand me?"

I didn't nod. I didn't move. The guy didn't like that.

He turned to the other man. "Bag him."

That sent a jolt through me. Bag me? I quickly found out what that meant. The other guy brought out a thick black hood, tugged it forcefully over my head, and pulled it tightly to my throat with a string. I could see nothing. Then they flipped me over, yanked both my hands behind my back, and bound them together with what sounded like some kind of heavy-duty zip tie. I wondered if I was going to be shot dead at any moment. Was this where it all ended? I was suddenly facing the devastating truth that I would likely never see Ashley and Joy again.

They yanked me to my feet, dragged me out onto the walkway in front of my motel room. Where were they taking me? Was I about to be tortured or worse? Were these guys working for Pullson? They jerked me forward, my feet stumbling along because I couldn't see anything. I think we were moving toward the parking lot. Could anyone at the motel see what was happening? Should I scream for help? Before I could, I heard a sliding door being pulled open. And then I was basically tossed into a vehicle, where my face slammed against the metal floor. It felt like my skull cracked. Was this a van? It had to be a van of some sort. The door was slammed shut behind me. I heard the front doors both open and close. The engine roared to life, and the vehicle's tires squealed as the gas was punched. The driver did a swift turn, which made me slide hard into a side metal wall. More turning, more sliding and banging my head and body all around.

"Where are you taking me?" I asked.

They didn't respond. I could hear other vehicles around us on the street now. Someone had their music pumping loudly. I had to find a way out of this. I couldn't let it end this way. I had come way too far to fail now.

"Whatever you're being paid, I'll triple it," I yelled at them.

"Shut the hell up!" one of the guys said.

But I didn't shut up. I was desperate. "I'll give you a million dollars if you let me go right now. We can go straight to the bank and have it wired into your account."

I heard movement. Sounded like one of the guys was shifting into the back with me. Had my offer worked? I quickly found out it had not. The guy kicked me hard in the gut, causing my insides to turn and every last bit of breath to rush out of my covered mouth.

"I told you to shut up!" he said.

Then I heard him return to his front passenger seat. It was clear I was not going to be able to bribe these guys. While trying to recover from the blow of his shoe, I tried to think of another alternative to get out of this situation. But I had nothing. This thing was going to the worst place possible—maybe my death—and I could do nothing about it.

Then I felt the violent impact of another vehicle, which caused cursing up front and the van to swerve hard. I was tossed up into the air before I collided with the opposite side of our vehicle. What the hell had just happened? Our vehicle was continuing to swerve wildly, as if the driver couldn't regain control, before I felt us hit something dead-on. I heard metal crunch, glass shatter, as I went flying forward. I smashed up hard against what felt like the back of one of the van's chairs. I heard grunting and moaning up front. The two guys must've been badly battered themselves. The van had come to a sudden stop. Then I heard the back door slide open. Someone jumped inside the vehicle with me. Seconds later, my hood was yanked off my head.

I stared up at the guy's face, shocked.

Nick Cantley. Former CIA agent.

Before I could say anything, he spun me around, cut away my zip tie, and freed my hands. I glanced toward the front of the van. The windshield was shattered. Neither of my captors wore their ski masks. The guy in the driver's seat was lying forward on the steering wheel, as if he might be knocked out. The passenger seat guy held both hands in front of him, staring at them, because they were covered in blood.

"What's going on?" I managed to ask Nick.

"Later," he said. "Let's go!"

He pulled me up, and I followed him out of the van. We were in the middle of a warehouse district somewhere. I could see a black

Tahoe with a smashed front right bumper parked right in front of the van. Nick must've been driving that. He had to have been following us.

I took one step forward, felt a shooting pain in my knee, and then fell to the pavement. I caught myself with my hands before busting my skull again. My knee must've gotten banged up when my body was being ping-ponged around the back of the van.

Nick knelt in front of me. "You okay? Can you move?"

"What choice do I have?" I asked, trying to push myself up.

"None. So let's get the hell out of here."

But we didn't get that chance. The guy in the passenger seat of the van popped out and immediately charged at Nick, who was vulnerable in his kneeling position. The guy tackled the former CIA agent, sending both tumbling to the pavement. My captor was much bigger than Nick, who seemed dazed by the impact. The guy wrapped his massive right arm around Nick's neck and started choking him. I had to do something quick, or the guy who had just saved me was going to get taken out himself. I pushed myself up onto my wobbly knee, grimaced with each step, and then launched myself forward, like I was diving into a swimming pool. I held my elbow out like a weapon and put it right in my captor's ear, causing his head to whip sideways and his grip to loosen on Nick. I rolled several times on the pavement. The impact was enough to free Nick, who bolted to his feet, moved on top of the staggered guy, and put a knee straight into his nose. I heard something crack as the guy's head was tossed back, and blood splattered. The guy collapsed to the pavement, holding his battered face, moaning in agony.

Nick then grabbed me by the shirt, yanked me up. I wrapped my arm around his shoulder, as we both moved as swiftly as possible down the sidewalk, around the crunched-up van, and over to his Tahoe. I peered back and could see my other captor now stirring awake inside the van. That guy was even bigger than the one down on the pavement behind us. I didn't really want another tussle. And it appeared Nick didn't want it, either. He opened the passenger door to the Tahoe, shoved me inside, circled around.

Seconds later, Nick had the pedal down and the SUV rocketed forward.

THIRTY-SEVEN

After zigzagging through the city, we parked in an alley somewhere off the beaten path, got out, and Nick opened a back door to an old three-story brick building. I followed him inside. It was a simple room the size of an efficiency apartment, with concrete floors and no windows. There was a twin-size bed in one corner, a sofa with a small TV on a stand, a refrigerator, and a square wooden table with four folding chairs around it. There also looked to be a bathroom in the corner of the room.

"Where are we?" I asked him.

"Safe house," Nick replied.

"A CIA safe house?"

"Correct."

"I thought you didn't work for the CIA anymore."

"I don't. But I didn't turn in all my keys." He nodded toward the square table with the chairs. "Why don't you have a seat? We have a lot to talk about."

"You can say that again."

I hobbled over to the table, pulled out a chair, and sat.

"Are you okay?" Nick asked me.

"Hell no, I'm freaking out."

"I mean physically."

"I don't know. My knee is throbbing. My shoulder hurts like hell. I feel like I just went twelve rounds with Mike Tyson. But other than that, I'm okay."

"You want some water or something?" he asked me.

"No, I'm good."

"I might have beer in the fridge."

"Will you just tell me what's going on?"

"It's your day of reckoning."

I frowned. "What the hell does that mean?"

"You'll see." He walked over to the fridge, opened it, grabbed a bottle of beer. "You sure you don't want one?"

"Yes."

He popped his open with his pocketknife, downed a gulp. It was clear Nick was going to get into this when he was damn well ready.

"Since you asked about the CIA, I presume you already know my name?"

"Nick Cantley—Falls Church, Virginia. Worked for the CIA for eight years. No longer employed there as of four years ago."

"Impressive."

I said, "I guess I should thank you for saving my ass back there."

"They weren't going to kill you. They were just trying to scare you."

"Well, it was working. So thanks."

"No problem. Thanks for returning the favor."

"Who were they?"

"Contracted ex-military thugs sent by Pullson."

"Are you serious?"

"You put yourself in a bad situation today."

"I'm flying blind here. So help me out."

He found a seat in a folding chair across the table from me. "First off, you should know that Ashley and Joy are okay."

That nearly made me bolt out of my chair. "How do you know that?"

"I'm sort of friends with Ashley."

I'd been carrying around the worst fear imaginable ever since Ashley had disappeared, that something awful had happened to them. I'd even pondered their deaths in my darkest moments. To hear him say they were okay flooded my whole body with relief. But could I trust this guy? I was still so confused.

My forehead wrinkled. "'Sort of'?"

"It's a long-ass story, Luke."

"Did she send you to our house to get the money from the safe?"

"Yes. She had nothing and desperately needed it. I volunteered to go get it. Sorry for what happened. Your jaw okay?"

"It's fine. How do you know my wife?"

He sighed. "Because I'm the one who got her out of China alive."

I was stunned to hear that. "Where are they?"

"They're safe. That's all you need to know right now."

"Safe from who? Who's behind all of this?"

"I think you already know that. You've been a very busy man the past couple of days."

"You've been tracking me?"

"Yes."

"Why?"

"For your own safety."

"So the Chinese government is behind all of this?"

"Not exactly. More specifically a high-ranking security detail working directly for Chen Liu, the US ambassador for China. And led by a man named Zhao Ming."

"Chang," I muttered.

He squinted at me. "Who?"

"I've been calling him Chang because back in Vail he told me he was Special Agent Chang with the FBI."

"I see."

"Did this Zhao Ming kill Danny Lamar from the FBI?"

"I'm afraid so."

"Because of me?"

"You can't blame yourself, Luke. You didn't know. Ming must've thought you pulling in the FBI would be bad for their pursuit of Ashley."

"Ming also killed Ashley's mother, Janny Bowman?"

"Yes."

"And Kai Lin in Laguna Beach?"

"Correct. They were all threats."

"Why didn't he kill me?"

"Because you are the best bait they have left."

I cursed. "How do you know all of this?"

"I've been with Ashley the whole time."

"Why?"

"This is where I start at the beginning, I guess."

"Please do."

He took another long swig of his beer, finished it off. "As you now know, Ashley was originally Sarah Bowman, who was arrested doing missionary work in China six years ago. Obviously, she didn't die in a jailhouse. A lieutenant colonel in the Chinese military took Sarah and pushed forward the official death mirage. Then he put up a wall around the truth, even from his own government."

"Is that even possible?"

"It's China, man. Anything is possible."

"Why did he take Sarah?"

"Sarah walked in on him raping one of the teenage girls she'd been evangelizing in the village where she'd been staying. So he immediately detained her and basically kept her in private captivity inside his own wall-enclosed property for about six months. Sarah had no exposure to the outside world. No one knew she was even there except a couple of his top military leaders."

I swallowed. "Did he, you know . . ."

"I never felt like I should ask Sarah that question."

I nodded. "So how did she get out?"

"His two young daughters inadvertently discovered her one day and became enthralled with her. So the colonel let her out of her jail cell but kept her guarded inside the property. Sarah became a private tutor for his daughters because he thought it would be valuable for them to learn English and the ways of the US from an actual American. But she was never allowed on the internet or outside the property. So she had no clue what had been reported about her back in the States. At least, at first."

"What changed?"

"She met Han Liu."

"Assistant vice minister of foreign affairs?"

"Correct. Liu was friendly with the lieutenant colonel and was over at his house one day when he spotted Sarah working in the garden with the two girls. Liu was captivated by her from the first moment he met her. He started coming around more, trying to get more time with her. Sarah was friendly. She was trying to make the best of her situation. She was no longer treated badly in the home. Even though she was placed under constant security, as to not run away, she was otherwise taken good care of. The little girls had no clue she was an actual prisoner. And Sarah never treated them like she was. She grew to love those little girls and poured everything she had into them."

That sounded just like Ashley, always making good from bad. "What happened between Sarah and Han Liu?"

"They grew closer over time. Since he was a trusted government official and the colonel wanted his favor, Liu was allowed free access to Sarah. So they began spending a lot of time together on the property. Sarah also became somewhat infatuated with Liu. He was very kind to her. And he also acknowledged her unfortunate situation and showed her empathy. And then the big event happened."

"What big event?"

"Han Liu secretly became a Christian. Sarah had been constantly sharing her faith with him and privately taking him through the Bible. Han Liu immediately had an impossible situation on his hands. There was no way he could come out publicly as a Christian. He was certain to lose his position with the government and possibly way worse, since it would shine such a negative light on his father's role as the US ambassador. So he kept it private. But the religious conversion only strengthened the bond between Sarah and Liu. Soon they were in love—without a single other person knowing about it. They even decided to secretly get married. Liu snuck in an underground house church pastor by claiming he was a special government assistant in his department. The three of them did it in the garden."

I thought about the photo I'd found of the two of them together. The one with Ashley holding the red roses. It was indeed a wedding photo. But I could have never imagined how it had come about.

"What happened next?"

"Han Liu felt trapped in prison himself and was not okay with it. He obviously did not want his wife living in captivity away from him. So through back channels he reached out to Senator Pullson, whom he'd met several times on Pullson's trips to China, for help. Liu wanted to somehow escape China with Sarah and come to the States. But he knew that was no easy task. First, Liu couldn't get her out all by himself. He also knew they would have to start all over once they got to the US. That meant new names and everything. Because it was highly unlikely the Chinese were going to simply let him walk away without consequences. Liu knew too much. He struck a deal with Pullson: if Liu got help getting both him and Sarah out and set up with a new life, he would share valuable intelligence information with Pullson."

This story kept building. I was on the edge of my seat. "Maybe I will have that beer," I told him.

He smiled, got up. He returned with two cold bottles and popped the tops off both, then slid one over to me. I took a swig.

"Is this where you came into the story?" I asked.

"Yes. Because Pullson had been head of the CIA, he still had all kinds of private pull with the agency. I got recruited onto a small offline elite covert team assigned to the task. We created a plan to go into China and bring them both home. We were on-site and getting ready for the assignment when everything blew up on us."

"How did it blow up?"

"Liu's father, Chen Liu, somehow found out what was happening. He confronted his son, who told him the truth. About his religious conversion and his secret marriage to Sarah—all of it. Chen Liu was obviously irate. Threats were made through certain channels from Chen Liu to Senator Pullson, so Pullson immediately made the call to abort the entire operation. He didn't want his hands getting dirty. He had too much at stake with China. My team immediately packed it up and bolted."

"But you stayed?"

He sighed, nodded. "I got word from a local that Han Liu had been shot dead. Orders given directly from his own father. I guess Chen Liu knew his career would be destroyed if word ever got out about what his son had done. He wasn't going to let that happen. I knew Sarah was next. They would certainly kill her. Pullson had basically signed her death orders. I couldn't let it happen."

"You got her out all by yourself?"

"No. I'd done other operations in China, so I had some of my own local mercenary contacts. I quickly pulled together a ragtag team. Somehow, we got the job done. But it wasn't easy. A couple of the guys didn't make it out. But I tell you what, Sarah's the bravest woman I've ever met. She rolled with every underground maneuver we had to make. It took us two weeks of shadow play to finally sneak out of China. But we did it."

"Pullson know what you did?"

He shook his head. "No one did. Not even the other guys on my CIA special ops team. I made sure of that. I knew it would be a disaster for both me and Sarah. Pullson used his power to make sure the operation was never on the CIA books, as if Sarah Bowman never even existed. So it all just went away. Once we were back in the US, I got Sarah set up with a new identity and some money to get her new life started. But I told her for her own safety she could never tell anyone what had happened. It was obviously a brutal situation for her. Her husband had just been executed. The new life she'd hoped to be starting with him was dead. *And* she was pregnant."

"Did Han Liu know she was pregnant?"

"Yes, he'd brought her a pregnancy test to confirm it a few days before all hell broke loose. Unfortunately, that same pregnancy test was discovered and passed along to Han Liu's father. I got word through my Chinese network that Chen Liu was dead set on finding Sarah and taking the baby when it was born. It was his only remaining connection to his son, so he was determined to do whatever it took to get the child back."

"And that's how Ashley started her life on the run."

"Correct."

I could barely process everything—Ashley had been through hell and back. And she was still going through it.

"Why did you leave the CIA?" I asked him.

"After Sarah, I couldn't stomach it anymore. So I walked away. I've been doing private security consulting for international companies ever since."

"And you've been the one helping Sarah with all of the new IDs each step of the way?"

He nodded. "We've kept up with each other through an encrypted website. I tried to get Sarah to go to a remote part of the world, where Chen Liu would likely never find her. But she was adamant that she wanted a normal life with her daughter in the United States. She wouldn't leave, and it nearly cost her dearly a couple of times. Colorado was the longest stint she had without any issues. And then she met you."

"I became an issue?"

"For me, you did. I tried to talk Sarah—or Ashley, as you know her—out of marrying you. I told her it would only complicate matters for her protecting her real identity and potentially put her more at risk. I was insistent it wasn't worth it. But she couldn't walk away from you. She was in love with you, man. She risked it all to be with you."

That truth hit me so hard. I'd had no idea the enormity of the obstacle Ashley had to overcome to marry me. It went way beyond childhood abandonment issues.

"Was she ever going to tell me the truth?" I asked.

"Yes. Against my very strong advice. She said she could no longer keep secrets from you. You needed to know the truth. I think she was getting close to telling you when all of this blew up after that video of her rescuing those kids was released."

"That's how they found her?"

"The story went national. They are always watching. Their vast network has eyes everywhere."

"You came to Vail to help her?"

"Yes, right away. She was completely panicked."

"Did she immediately leave town?"

He shook his head. "Not at first. She was hoping things might somehow settle on their own. She did not want to leave you."

"But then I went and placed a huge target directly on her by doing that stupid TV show."

"Yep. She had no choice but to leave after that."

I cursed at myself. I thought about my first day searching for her in Vail Village. It had been Ashley I saw on the sidewalk outside the restaurant. She'd wanted to stay. But then I gave her no choice but to run.

"Don't beat yourself up too much. You were doing the best you could under circumstances you couldn't possibly understand."

"So where is she now?"

"I can't tell you that."

I glared at him. "Why the hell not?"

"Because you have a choice to make."

My forehead bunched. "What kind of choice?"

"The way I see it, you have two options. Option A, you can go back home to Vail, forget all of this happened, and move on with your life. If you drop this now, I think there's a good chance the Chinese will leave you alone. Don't get me wrong, they'll watch you. Like I said, you're bait. And they'll hope Ashley one day comes back for the bait. But you'll get to keep your big house and your successful career. You get to keep it all."

Did any of that really matter without Ashley and Joy?

"What's my other option?"

"We leave right now without a single word to anyone in your world. You disappear completely. And you never ever come back."

"But I get to be with Ashley?"

He nodded.

"How do you know she even wants me wherever she is?"

"I wouldn't be here if she didn't."

That was a relief to hear. Because I was beginning to dread Nick ending this conversation by telling me—even though Ashley was okay—I could never see her again. And that was by Ashley's choice. But she still wanted us to be together. And I wanted that more than anything.

"But here's the deal, Luke," Nick continued. "You can never have the same life you have here. You can't pursue a career like you have now. You can't have any type of job that might bring attention on yourself, which means you'll probably be barely getting by from here on out. That's your new life. And Ashley told me how hard you worked for your current life of affluence. It's a lot to give up."

"I have private offshore accounts."

"You can't access them. You'll leave a trail." He took a pull of his beer. "Ashley will understand if you choose to stay. She knows you didn't sign up for this kind of life. She was hesitant to even put this before you. But, like I said, she loves you. Personally, I think she's better off without you. But I promised her I would have this conversation with you."

"What about justice for all of this? Pullson? The Chinese?"

"Don't be naive. China is a different world. There is no justice to be had. Not without sealing your own fate. Ashley understood and accepted that. She believed God would eventually bring his own kind of justice."

This was surreal. I'd never even considered this could be my potential reality—to walk away from everything. I'd always envisioned bringing Ashley and Joy back home with me. My mind immediately reflected on the conversation we had on the night she agreed to marry me. Now I knew exactly what she meant.

"Would you leave behind everything for me?" she asked. "All of this, Luke. The house, the lifestyle, all of it."

"Why are you—"

"Please just tell me the truth."

"Of course I would."

"Are you sure? Be certain. Would you move across the world for me?"

"Ashley, what—"

"Just tell me."

"Yes, the answer is one hundred percent yes."

"What if we had to live in a shack in the woods?"

I had so many questions, but now was clearly not the time. "I'd go anywhere to be with you and Joy. I promise. I'd choose us. Always."

There was only one option. Home was with them.

I'd meant it then. And I meant it now.

THIRTY-EIGHT

Seven days later

I drove a rusted, run-down Honda Civic over an isolated dirt road through a jungle. It was more like a dirt path than an actual road. I had arrived on this small remote island only twenty minutes ago by pontoon plane. Nick had told me there were about a thousand locals on the island and most of them didn't speak a word of English. I would have to learn a new language. There was no internet or cell coverage on the island. To get access to any of that, or even groceries and other household items, I would need to take a boat forty-five minutes across the water to a bigger town on another island.

It had taken a full week to get here—probably the longest of my entire life. Nick had wanted to be so careful with each step of the way. It was a strange thing to disappear in a moment. It took me several days to get used to not having my phone constantly on me. It was like I'd lost an appendage or something. Nick had traveled with me most of the way. He said goodbye to me at the last stop before I got on the wobbly plane. I had nothing with me other than the clothes I was wearing, and a couple hundred dollars Nick had stuck in my pocket. He had arranged the Civic, too.

I was really starting completely over.

New name and everything.

And I had never been more excited.

A couple of more bumpy twists and turns on the dirt path before I pulled up to a beach with gorgeous blue water on the other side. I parked close to the sand, got out, smelled the clean salty air. From this side of the island, I couldn't see anything beyond the ocean. It was just blue water forever. I looked over to my left and found a walking path. I pulled out the scribbled directions Nick had given me. This was the correct path. I walked in that direction. My knee was still sore but was starting to feel better. I cut through green jungle for about fifty yards before it opened again onto another stretch of beautiful beach. There were about ten small huts built along the shore. I doubted any of them were bigger than eight hundred square feet. I could see what was likely a native woman with dark skin wearing a T-shirt and a bright-yellow skirt playing with a little girl outside the first hut. The girl was probably around Joy's age. This made me smile. I hadn't stopped smiling since I got on the pontoon plane thirty minutes ago, knowing this was my final stop.

I took off my running shoes, stepped onto the beach, the soft white sand squirting through my toes, and walked past the first couple of huts. They all looked sturdy and well built. Most of them had little front porches with ocean views. There were no visible electrical lines anywhere. What was life like without TV, phones, and internet? I was about to find out. In some ways, it felt intimidating. I had been so connected for so long. But it also felt like freedom. A freedom I thought I'd longed to have for some time now.

My eyes were set on the very last hut. I could feel myself getting nervous. Did Ashley really want me here? Nick said she did, but I couldn't know the full truth without seeing it for myself.

Then she appeared on the tiny front porch of her hut. She didn't notice me at first, her eyes locked on the ocean. She was a vision. She had not changed her appearance this time. Her hair was still dark, curly, and long. Maybe she didn't feel like it was necessary since she'd made this dramatic of a move so far away from the United States. She wore a white cotton sundress and was barefoot. Her skin was tanned and glowing. She had never looked more beautiful. I could feel my heart pounding. Tears hit my eyes, and I tried to force them back. I didn't need to be a crying idiot when she finally noticed me. But I could hardly help myself. I'd thought I'd lost her and Joy forever. But now I'd found them.

She finally looked over, spotted me, dropped whatever item she was holding in her hand. Her mouth parted; her eyes grew wide. She looked like she'd seen a ghost, as if she wasn't sure she could believe her own eyes. Nick hadn't told her I was coming. He didn't want any unnecessary communication. Then she hesitantly stepped off the porch into the sand. We both just stood for a second, thirty feet apart, taking in this moment.

Then she smiled so purely that her entire face flushed with color. She ran to me, closing the gap quickly, and we threw our arms around each other. I had my answer. I pulled her in so tight I was afraid I might crack one of her ribs. I spun her around once, her feet off the ground, and then finally set her back down. Our lips connected, as I held her face in my trembling hands.

"I can't believe you're here," she said, staring up at me.

"I made a promise to you."

"I know. But . . . I wasn't sure. You didn't know everything back then."

"I do now. And I'm still here."

Her eyes were watering. So were mine. We kissed again, holding each other so close, neither of us wanting to ever let go again. It took a three-year-old bundle of joy to pull me away from Ashley.

"Luke!" Joy squealed from the porch.

We both turned. Joy was in a pink one-piece swimsuit. She leaped off the porch into the sand and sprinted toward me. I scooped her up, hugged her, and spun her in the air several times.

"I'm so happy to see you, sweetheart," I said.

"I've missed you *so much*," Joy said.

My stepdaughter was crying now. We were all crying. But these were tears of relief. Tears of hope. Tears for the future. Our future together. Ashley moved into the circle with us, and we all hugged each other. I didn't know how we would survive. I had no clue what kind of work or job I would do around here. But none of that mattered right now. We would figure it out. All that mattered was that we were finally a family again.

We were finally home.

ABOUT THE AUTHOR

Photo © 2019 Amy Melsa

Chad Zunker is the Amazon Charts bestselling author of *All He Has Left* and *Family Money*, as well as the David Adams series, including *An Equal Justice*, which was nominated for the 2020 Harper Lee Prize for Legal Fiction; *An Unequal Defense*; and *Runaway Justice*. Chad also penned *The Tracker*, *Shadow Shepherd*, and *Hunt the Lion* in the Sam Callahan series. He studied journalism at the University of Texas, where he was also on the football team. Chad has worked for some of the country's most powerful law firms and has also invented baby products that are sold all over the world. He lives in Austin with his wife, Katie, and their three daughters and is hard at work on his next novel. For more information, visit www.chadzunker.com.